PRAISE FOR THE DAVID GRAHAM MYSTERY SERIES

"Bravo! Engrossing!"
"I'm in love with him and his colleagues."
"A terrific mystery."
"These books certainly have the potential to become a PBS series with the likeable character of Inspector Graham and his fellow officers."
"Delightful writing that keeps moving, never a dull moment."
"I know I have a winner of a book when I toss and turn at night worrying about how the characters are doing."
"Love it and love the author."
"Refreshingly unique and so well written."
"Solid proof that a book can rely on good

storytelling and good writing without needing blood or sex."

"This series just gets better and better."

"DI Graham is wonderful and his old school way of doing things, charming."

"Great character development."

"Kept me entertained all day."

"Please write more!"

THE CASE OF THE FALLEN HERO

BOOKS IN THE INSPECTOR DAVID GRAHAM SERIES

Visit the link below for all my large print editions:

www.alisongolden.com/large-print

LARGE PRINT PAPERBACKS

The Case of the Screaming Beauty

The Case of the Hidden Flame

The Case of the Fallen Hero

The Case of the Broken Doll

The Case of the Missing Letter

The Case of the Pretty Lady

The Case of the Forsaken Child

The Case of Sampson's Leap

The Case of the Uncommon Witness

COLLECTIONS

(*regular print only*)

Books 1-4

The Case of the Screaming Beauty

The Case of the Hidden Flame

The Case of the Fallen Hero

The Case of the Broken Doll

Books 5-7

The Case of the Missing Letter

The Case of the Pretty Lady

The Case of the Forsaken Child

THE CASE OF THE FALLEN HERO

ALISON GOLDEN

GRACE DAGNALL

Cover illustration: Richard Eijkenbroek

Published by Mesa Verde Publishing
P.O. Box 1002
San Carlos, CA 94070

ISBN: 979-8862346336

"Books give a soul to the universe, wings to the mind, flight to the imagination, and life to everything."
- Plato -

"Your emails seem to come on days when I need to read them because they are so upbeat."
- Linda W -

For a limited time, you can get the first books in each of my series - *Chaos in Cambridge, Hunted* (exclusively for subscribers - not available anywhere else), *The Case of the Screaming Beauty, and Mardi Gras Madness* - plus updates about new releases, promotions, and other Insider exclusives, by signing up for my mailing list at:

https://www.alisongolden.com/graham

PROLOGUE
ORGUEIL CASTLE, NEAR GOREY, JERSEY

Saturday, 3:30 p.m.
THE FOUR FRIENDS tumbled out of the minivan, thanked their driver, and stared agog at the imposing medieval castle that now towered over them.

"Bloody hell," Harry managed, wiping his glasses clean and staring at the immense walls. "It's *big,* isn't it?"

Emily retrieved her priceless violin from the van's back seat and joined him, looking up at the impenetrable, solid battlements that spoke of the castle's deep history. "Going for your Masters in Architecture, Harry?" she joked. "It's an eight hundred-year-old *fortress.* I don't think *big* does it justice."

Harry made sure his already-battered cello case had suffered no additional indignities on the ferry ride over from Weymouth and hoisted its weight onto his shoulder with well-practiced ease. "Well, I wouldn't dream of upstaging our resident expert."

Leo Turner-Price, a twig-like specimen of a man with a shock of brown hair stood a few feet away. An accomplished historian and violinist, he stared at the castle as though achieving a lifelong dream. "Emily is right about the structure being eight *centuries* old. But there are records of substantial fortifications that go back to the Bronze Age."

"Really?" Harry remarked. "Wow."

"All to keep out the beastly French," Marina observed. The youngest of the four members of the Spire String Quartet, Marina was a shy but—as Harry once described her in an unguarded moment —"insanely attractive" viola player who taught young children at two of London's most expensive schools. "Must have cost a fortune."

"Well, if that was their aim," Harry opined, keeping up his role as the "bluff Brit abroad," "it was money well spent."

Emily flicked her ponytail off her shoulders and rolled her eyes. Fifteen years into her friendship with the wonderfully gruff plentifully bearded Harry Tringham, she found that he was still learning how to filter the thoughts that entered his overactive brain, far too many of which were given free passage direct to his equally active mouth. She spotted the visitors entrance up some steps in front of them. "Shall we?"

Emily was the only member of the quartet to have visited Orgueil Castle before, or even to have performed on the island of Jersey. It was through her contact with the castle's highly professional events manager, Stephen Jeffries, that they had been booked for the evening's wedding festivities. Always in need of a dependable ensemble who could provide light background music one moment and a strident processional the next, Jeffries kept Emily's name at the top of his hiring list.

He had been heartily impressed when, during a wedding two years before, Emily had led a young string trio through various weather-related disasters, a collapsed marquee, and a bridal arrival so delayed that the groom was harbouring the gravest of doubts. Having navigated these obstacles, Emily still possessed the presence of mind to guide her fellow musicians through a beautifully polished *Prince of Denmark's March* as the sodden bride entered, still dripping, into the Great Hall.

"Emily, my *darling!*" Jeffries exclaimed as he walked out to greet them. "*So* lovely to see you! How's your teaching going? Didn't you just start at that exclusive little prep school?" Like Marina,

Emily eked out her performance income with teaching.

"Fine, fine," Emily told him. "It's going well. Some of the little blighters even practice before their lessons." The whole quartet nodded. Finding students who were prepared to work hard was like finding gemstones in the desert. "It's nice to get a break though, and a change of scenery."

"Better weather for this one, too, eh?" Jeffries said, hand aloft toward the bluest possible sky.

"Much better," Emily agreed. "And I want to thank you for this, Stephen. Gives us all a pleasant break from an unseasonably warm London. This is Marina Linton," she said as the tall blonde extended a graceful hand. "Harry Tringham, our cellist, and resident physicist," she added, "and the historian Leo Turner-Price."

"Delighted to be here," Leo enthused. "Remarkable building, really."

Jeffries led them into an open quadrangle, home in part to a beautifully kept maze, and then down some steps into the castle's administrative area. Here they would relax and tune up until the wedding guests began arriving at five o'clock. Stephen moved paperwork and wedding paraphernalia off his biggest table to give them a safe, flat surface for their priceless instruments.

"Okay, did everyone's folders survive the journey?" Emily wanted to confirm. She received a trio of nods in reply. "Excellent," she said, quickly untying and retying her curly, black hair into a tighter ponytail. "So, we'll start with the little Baroque set..."

"Couperin," Harry said, finding the sheet music in his folder.

"And then the Purcell theatre music?" Marina asked.

"That's right. Then *Eine Kleine*. Everyone loves that," Emily said.

"All four movements?" Leo asked.

Emily thought for a second. "Let's play it by ear. Depends on timings and such, but we can axe the repeats if we need to hurry things along."

"Righto," Leo said, slotting his sheet music in the correct order. "Which processional did they choose in the end?"

Marina clasped both hands together, as if in prayer. "*Please* tell me it isn't Wagner again. I promised I'd quit weddings if I ever had to..."

"Nope," Emily reassured her. "*The Arrival of the Queen of Sheba.*"

All four sighed. "It's a terrific piece," Leo allowed, "but too much of a gallop for a processional, surely?"

Emily found the music and finished organising her folder. "She's the bride, Leo. And it's her..."

"*Special day!*" the three other members of the quartet chorused. They laughed together.

Jeffries watched this polished routine with un-concealed envy. "Honestly," he said as the four musicians finalised their folders, "I would simply *die* to make every aspect of these weddings as smooth as working with you guys."

"Aw, Stephen. You're an angel," Emily replied, kissing him on the cheek.

"I've already had a run-in with the mother of the bride," Jeffries admitted, his face relating just how ugly the encounter had been. "*Terrifying* woman. A foot wider than I am," he confessed, "and with a decidedly mean streak. These people get it into their heads that just because they've spent a fortune getting their offspring hitched, they can treat people *however they like!*"

Jeffries was a stylish and experienced man, un-used to brusque treatment. He allowed that the bridal party was under considerable pressure to en-sure their lovely daughter's wedding day was as close to perfect as possible, but still, their discour-tesy toward him seemed so unnecessary, especially when he was doing his level best to meet their every need.

"I'll leave you to it. Yell if you need anything," Jeffries said with a companionable hand on Emily's forearm. With a dramatic flourish, he then left to supervise the preparation of the reception.

Emily's preference was to start playing even before the guests arrived, ostensibly to create the "right atmosphere," but more practically to check acoustics and intonation. The quartet seated themselves in one corner of the quadrangle where the marquee—the same one that had suffered the spectacular structural failure during Emily's last performance at the castle—was set up. Guests would shortly be wandering on the lawn of the quad, ducking inside to grab a drink or a canapé, and rubbing shoulders before the bridal party arrived.

As they waited, the group rehearsed their plan. They talked quietly in the short gaps between movements of the tasteful Couperin suite Harry had arranged for them years before. Once it was confirmed that the bride was ready to go through with the ceremony (and in Emily's ten-year experience of weddings, this was by no means an absolute certainty,) the quartet would have only a few moments to quickly relocate to the Great Hall and prepare for the processional.

Later, after the bride reached the altar, the musicians' time would be their own. Jeffries would hand them a generous cheque, and they'd enjoy the rest of the evening before retreating to a local hostel for the night. The castle would then play host to an extended party before the guests collapsed into bed. There was plentiful accommodation within the giant edifice so that, as Jeffries always thought of it, they wouldn't have to stagger far.

"Let's skip the minor-key Purcell movements," Marina said. "I don't feel like playing in D-minor under a sky as beautiful as this." The quartet unanimously agreed and launched into the joyously dotted rhythms of Purcell's more animated theatre pieces. The eighty or so guests were now arriving in a steady stream, and the quadrangle filled with music, the clink of wine glasses, and old friends catching up after too long apart.

Their intonation perfect and their balance as tightly controlled as ever, the quartet revelled playing simply for fun. After the second movement of *Eine Kleine Nachtmusik*, Harry leant over to Marina and grinned. "Doesn't feel like work, does it?"

"Not even a little bit," she said, following Emily's lead for the beginning of the minuet.

An excitable Stephen Jeffries scuttled over. "She's *here!*" he announced in a boisterous whisper. "Action stations!"

Emily used eye contact alone—as the best leaders can—to bring the minuet to a quick but elegant halt, and the quartet made their way to the Great Hall slightly ahead of the politely ushered guests. Moments later, the ravishing Marie Joubert —soon to be Marie Ross—stepped steadily and confidently down the aisle in her white lace gown with its elaborate train, the filigree of Handel, and the beaming smiles of her family accompanying her as she walked.

CHAPTER ONE

H OW ARE YOU settling in to your new room, sir?" Polly asked. The White House Inn's breakfast server leant over to pour Detective Inspector David Graham a cup of tea.

He turned to her and beamed. "Very nicely, Polly. Very nicely, indeed, thank you. You and all the staff here do Mrs. Taylor proud."

After a substantial and satisfying breakfast, Graham inhaled the extremely promising cup of tea he'd just been poured. He relaxed in his window seat. The view, all the way to France on a morning as clear as this, calmed him. Small boats dotted the crystal blue waters of the English Channel, and despite the thickness of the hotel dining room's double-glazed windows, he could pick out the cry of seagulls as they wheeled in the sky.

Around a hundred small vessels were moored in Gorey's marina although some were already venturing out into the Channel. Graham, savouring the first sip of his tea much like a wine connoisseur appreciated a nicely aerated claret, watched the white canvas sails unfurl as a trio of small sailing craft made their way out of the harbour .

Life on Jersey had been good to Graham. He had lost perhaps five pounds since his arrival in Gorey despite Mrs. Taylor's massive, traditional breakfasts and the occasional Thai curry at the Bangkok Palace. He hadn't had a drink in over two months, not even on his thirty-sixth birthday which had passed quietly three weeks earlier.

The changes extended further. He had had his fair hair trimmed a little shorter, both for ease of maintenance and because he thought it gave him a slightly more polished appearance. His blue eyes were rediscovering their old twinkle, especially after a good, strong pot of Assam and a mile or so walk around Gorey. Mostly, he felt that the worst of the past and its many challenges were now behind him. Jersey's sea air, the change of environment, and the much-reduced workload were all doing him a world of good.

The home front was also nicely stable. Graham

had come to a most reasonable arrangement with Mrs. Taylor following his recent investigative success. Amidst the prospect of very unwelcome media attention for the hotel, Graham had swiftly solved the brutal murder of a White House Inn guest whose body was discovered on the beach below. Mrs. Taylor had chosen to express her gratitude by moving Graham to a better-appointed room at a heavily discounted rate.

When he'd first arrived on Jersey, Graham had planned to find a cottage or apartment as quickly as possible, but he found that he liked the inn enormously. The other guests were either long-termers like himself or were on vacation. Either way, it made for a relaxed atmosphere. The community that resided at the White House Inn was a genuine source of solace and enjoyment for Inspector Graham. He fell easily into conversations and made fast friends with many of the long-term guests, a welcome break from his police work. The food at the inn was excellent, some of the best on the island, and the chef found marvellous uses for the varied local seafood.

Mrs. Taylor's extensive selection of teas was uppermost in Graham's mind, though. In the dark days before his departure from London, Graham found himself leaning on tea. He had found it a surprising but effective crutch during his painful journey staving off a dependency on alcohol. Tragedy had driven him to the brink of despair, and as his marriage crumbled, Graham sought oblivion. Good friends, a superb physician, and the support of the Metropolitan Police had helped him pull through. However, once he'd cracked a murder case in his home village of Chiddlinghurst, just outside London, Graham found he could interest himself only in a quick and complete exit from the area and the painful memories it held for him.

Gorey, in welcome contrast, was proving idyllic, the murder at the inn six weeks before, not-withstanding. Under his direction, the other three full-time members of Gorey Constabulary, the tiny policing outpost responsible for public safety in this part of the Bailiwick of Jersey, were fast becoming highly competent officers. Graham allowed that Constable Barnwell was still something of a well-meaning oaf, but he was showing promise and drinking a lot less these days. Young Constable Roach was committed to his professional develop-ment and Graham couldn't ask for a more solid and dependable second-in-command than Sergeant Janice Harding. With her steady hand on the tiller, theirs was now a tightly run ship that had quickly gained a reputation as a hard-working and effective outfit.

Above all, Graham found time and time again,

tea kept him happy, alert, and content with his lot. As he sat looking out over the high clifftop to the blue sea and skies beyond, he noted to himself that there was little more he would demand of the world than a good pot of Assam and the incredible view.

But Graham wasn't a man to sit around all day. He'd made a point of visiting a number of the historical sites in Jersey and its excellent zoo. He was becoming something of an amateur historian of the area. The period of World War II during which Jersey was occupied by the Germans particularly interested him. He was fascinated by the old underground hospital with its built-in railway system, as well as the dozens of defensive positions and turrets that dotted the coastline and had comprised part of Hitler's Atlantic Wall back in the day.

And then there was Orgueil Castle—pronounced "Or-Goy"—the imposing medieval structure that watched over the town like a sleeping stone giant. Graham had visited it twice already, but he tended to find the place a little too crowded for his liking once the tour buses arrived. Visitors from the British mainland and France would swarm the castle at certain times of the day and to avoid them Graham planned to show up this morning right at opening time. Hopefully, he might have the place to himself, at least for a short while.

A shuttle bus ran through the town, but it didn't

run this early on a Sunday, so Graham decided to walk. He finished his tea and rose from his table, glancing at his watch—only eight-fifteen. Not even churchgoers were out and about yet. The castle opened its doors at eight-thirty during these last weeks of the tourist season, and he hoped to be their first customer.

Ten minutes later, Graham reached the outside of the castle. The imposing monument was a complex pile of thick stones that straddled the line between function and elegance. Striding up the steep approach road to the entrance, Graham noticed signs of the repairs necessary to patch up the effects of weathering over many centuries. Some of the stones in the battlements sported a different, more recent colour. As he reached the main gate, Graham marvelled anew at the sheer immensity of the structure. The time and effort and expense it would have taken—all in pre-industrial times—to hew, transport, and assemble the rock that comprised the castle was incredible. The *decades* of craftsmanship required to build the fortification simply boggled the mind.

Apart from the sweeping battlements and their commanding views of Gorey, the Channel, and

France beyond, Graham's favourite parts of the castle were the passageways. Topped by thick, stone arches, these walkways burrowed their ways inside the castle. He never tired of strolling through them, imagining the heroics required to build the precise arches that rose above him. In the days before calculators and computers, an engineer was, by necessity, something of a genius.

Not for the first time, Graham noticed that there was barely a straight wall in the castle. He ran his eye along the lines. There must be some military advantage to be gained from constant turns and odd angles. He admired the beautifully kept maze and then headed back under the castle, following a passageway that ran by a huge bronze statue of a figure seated on horseback. It was then that he heard it.

For an experienced police officer, there is something compelling about a scream. This one was long, urgent, and panicked. A thrill of adrenaline swarmed Graham's body. He dashed toward the sound. Something terrible had happened and as he ran, he knew his plan for a relaxed Sunday was done for.

CHAPTER TWO

AS GRAHAM TURNED a corner, ahead of him he saw a woman on the stone walkway that ran beneath one of the taller castle battlements. Graham sprinted out of the dark passageway and into the courtyard where the woman knelt. She cradled a man lying at an unnatural angle, her brown hair brushing the man's lifeless face.

"Police, ma'am," Graham said, as he skidded to a halt a few feet from the couple. Taking a breath, he calmly approached and crouched next to the woman. She continued wailing, as though Graham were invisible, her hands under the stricken man's head. "I'm trained in first aid," Graham told her. "Let me help him."

Blood rushed onto the stone from at least one serious head wound. The man bled from both ears. From the awkward position of his hips and legs, Graham quickly assumed substantial fractures. "What happened?" He assessed the man's injuries, but the woman stared at the sky and continued to howl.

Graham gently moved her hands aside—they were covered in blood—and reached for a pulse. Finding nothing, he leant in to listen for breathing. Not even the slightest whisper or tremble reverberated against in his ear. "We need to get him to the hospital *immediately*," Graham told the woman, already certain in his own mind that medical help would prove futile, but willing to try.

Graham stood, his own shirt bloodied now. He reached for his phone to dial 999. "Graham, Gorey Constabulary," he told the operator. "I need an ambulance at Orgueil Castle immediately. A male, mid-thirties, appears to have fallen. He has serious injuries." He listened as the operator confirmed the details and promised an ambulance would be with him shortly.

The cessation of wailing and the sound of footsteps tapping on the stone walkway caught Graham's attention. His eyes widened as he caught sight of the woman fleeing down the stone path out of the castle grounds and toward Gorey, her light cotton dress flapping around her like the wings of a graceful bird preparing to take flight.

"Wait!" he shouted. "*Attendez-vous!*" he tried next, but the woman didn't falter and she ignored his pleas. "Well," Graham said, still slightly out of breath. "Well. Bugger."

The man at his feet, now almost certainly a *victim* of some kind, remained resolutely mute and inert. Graham crouched again and looked the body over once more. "What happened to you, eh? Was this what you planned when you got out of bed this morning?"

Attracted by the shouts, a few early risers who, like Graham had been strolling around the castle, arrived. "Please stay back!" Graham ordered.

A slight man with thick glasses and brown clothing that gave him the appearance of a barn owl cried out, "I say, is there anything we can do?"

Graham replied quietly, almost as though the injured man might hear, as he reached for his phone again. "I don't think so. This is a police matter now."

Stephen Jeffries, his face etched with horror and panic skidded to a stop next to Graham. He grabbed Graham's arm as the detective barred on-lookers from the body, imploring them not to take photos. "You're the police?" Jeffries asked. "S-Stephen Jeffries, castle events." He looked down at the man on the floor. "He was the groom. Married... only yesterday, only *hours* ago..." Jeffries squeaked. He gazed deep into Graham's eyes as though he could see the prior day's nuptials reflected in them. "Beautiful ceremony." Then it occurred to him. "Hell's teeth... his *wife*! Did someone tell her?"

"What does she look like?"

"Long brown hair, slim—like a reed really, tall. Marie Ross."

"Ah, then that was her. There was a woman with the body when I arrived, but she ran away. I called after her, but she ignored me. Perhaps overcome with grief." Graham put his phone to his ear.

"She ran?" Jeffries said, trying to piece together the scene. "Just *ran off*?"

"You'd be surprised how shock can affect a person," Graham told him. "I've seen people sprint away like Olympic gold medalists just seconds after getting the worst news of their lives despite never before having run a mile." His call went through. "Sergeant Harding?"

A very sleepy voice answered. "Boss?"

"I'm afraid so. Sorry to disturb your Sunday morning. Can you get over to the castle, right away?"

"Huh?" Harding struggled to sit up in bed.

"Body at the bottom of some ramparts. I'm..."

Graham heard a clatter. Harding had dropped her phone.

"Bloody hell, boss..." Harding muttered after a short delay. "I'm on my way."

"Harding?"

"Eh? I mean, yes, boss?"

"Get Tomlinson on the horn and make sure he's up and about as well, would you? We'll need the full works. You'll see for yourself how this looks, but if I've learnt anything in this business, it's not to judge a book by its cover. You know what I mean?"

"I do, boss," Harding answered, struggling into her uniform blouse. "I'll call him next. Be there soon."

Beside Graham, Jeffries wrung his hands. Two waiters from last night's wedding had volunteered to come in early to clean up. Now they covered the body with a pristine, white tablecloth. It remained perfect for mere seconds before inevitably staining red.

To Graham, one of the saddest tasks relating to a sudden death was the necessity of establishing identity. Beyond the bloodied remains now at his feet, he knew this young man had probably enjoyed a full life, had a cherished circle of friends, and a family who loved him. In this especially tragic case, he had a wife so new that the wedding guests had not yet dispersed. Rummaging through the man's clothing, he found a wallet in a trouser pocket.

"George Ross," Graham read. "Thirty years old." He shook his head sadly. "Not nearly good enough, old chap."

The remainder of the wallet's contents extended not much farther than the usual assortment of debit and credit cards, memberships to a couple of organisations, and store loyalty cards. Further rummaging uncovered a photo of his beloved, barely recognisable as the distraught woman who had wailed so inconsolably before vanishing into Gorey.

Running his fingers between the leather slots of the wallet, Graham found some cash in the form of the still, to him, unfamiliar Jersey banknotes, and in another pocket he uncovered a room key marked "Bridal Suite."

"Not a lot to go on," Graham muttered quietly. He set the wallet and license aside to await an evidence bag. He regarded the draped body again. "Thirty years old." He imagined himself at that age, also newly married, a baby in the planning stages, documents drawn up for a house purchase and requisite mortgage, a future of togetherness, promise and possibility ahead. He shook his head. "You poor sod," he said. "You ran right out of luck, didn't you?"

CHAPTER THREE

HARRY TRINGHAM CLUTCHED his very welcome—if slightly gritty—take-out coffee as though it were the Elixir of Life. He ambled up the final few steps to the castle's visitors centre. He was not used to early starts, especially on Sundays, and it showed.

"A little worse for wear?" Emily asked brightly. She was looking energetic and ready for adventure in hiking boots, jeans, a bright red blouse, and a colourful silk scarf.

"You give musicians access to what is billed as an 'open bar,'" Harry retorted, "and you expect them not to make liberal use of it?"

Leo grinned sheepishly. He wasn't exactly feeling a hundred percent either, having helped put

away some of the "spare" champagne from the previous evening's function with relish. "I always feel
like one of those 14th century troubadours," he said,
"accepting the scraps from the table as part pay-
ment for my musical services."

Emily finished organising their tickets at the visitors' desk and pooled their contributions to pay the
entry fee. "Here you go," she said, distributing the
tickets. "Now, children, remember to hold hands,
take only photos, and make sure you don't wander
off without telling a teacher."

"Yes, Miss," the others chorused and then gig-
gled as they always did. Having performed in a
good number of Europe's most fascinating cultural
centres over the years, it was a cherished routine of
theirs to visit local sites the day after their contrac-
tual obligations had been fulfilled. Visiting the
castle was just up their street.

Emily often thought that their quartet particularly suited ancient spaces, chapels, museums, old
libraries, and the like, having begun their days as a
student ensemble amidst the medieval splendour of
Oxford University. Although hailing from four different colleges, the quartet had formed an instant
bond, become a fixture on the local wedding and
event circuit, and even produced a couple of CDs
just after graduating. Then, "real life intervened,"
as Harry put it, sending Emily and Marina to Lon-

don, Harry to Cambridge, and Leo to the respected history department at the University of Warwick.

"Lead the way, Mister Historian," Marina told Leo.

Leo immediately led them down a passageway into the bowels of the castle, launching into his spiel with gusto. "Let me know if I get boring," he added after a long explanation of medieval building techniques.

"Sure will," Harry muttered but then smiled. There was a genuine affection between the members of the ensemble, which had survived the near-death experience of graduation from Oxford and their geographical dispersal, as well as more than one emotionally fraught "romantic complication," as Emily called them.

None of the four were yet married, and only Leo had been in a long-term relationship. Even that had faltered after his girlfriend, a scholar of Italian literature, had received an offer she couldn't refuse from a university in Milan. In more ways than the four were comfortable to admit, they were already in a complex and rewarding relationship—with music, with each other, the euphoria of their performances binding them—that was perhaps sufficient to ensure that none sought satisfaction elsewhere.

As they proceeded down the narrow tunnels of the castle's well-lit interior, sounds at the surface receded entirely. "Three feet thick," Leo told them, patting the cool stone of the passageway's walls. "Designed to withstand *years* of siege."

"I wish I were," Harry moaned. His hangover, the group's worst by some measure, was responding only sluggishly to the coffee and painkillers. "What is it about growing older that makes hangovers exponentially worse?"

Marina had the answer and she lectured Harry briskly on liver chemistry as they continued through the passageways. Leo bid them halt at an exhibit on the castle's history as a prison. Kingslayers and traitors had been given accommodation here, some as recently as four centuries ago before the island's jail was moved to a "newer" facility at St. Helier.

"Jesus, imagine being stuck down here in the dark," Emily wondered morbidly. "They'd have gone out of their minds."

Leo peered into the gloomy mock-up of a 16th century jail cell. "I don't know. They were made of pretty stern stuff back then. It's remarkable how spending a lifetime sitting on wooden benches or horseback toughens you up."

"How the hell would you know?" Harry sputtered. "You're just another pampered toff like the rest of us. When was the last time *you* were on *horseback*?"

Leo's impulse was to bristle and complain, but he considered Harry's fragile state. "Good point," he conceded, as the two women got a chuckle from the ham-fisted sparring of the two men.

Marina felt a little sorrier for Harry than she otherwise would. Their fling, only eighteen months ago, had turned out to be rather more complicated than she'd hoped. There had been some acrimony, but she still felt a lingering affection for him which surfaced more as care and concern than any romantic desire. Certainly, their tryst—known to the others as was their policy—had not been the quartet-shattering cataclysm Leo had predicted at the time. He'd made no such prophecy of doom, Marina noted when the tall, historically-inclined academic had asked her out a while earlier. Her refusal had sent Leo scuttling under a rock, and the quartet hadn't met for nearly four months, an unusually long hiatus.

"This was the magazine," Leo announced, gesturing to a vaulted space in the deepest part of the castle. The air was decidedly cool, a testament to the depth and the insulation provided by many feet of thick, ancient stone. "They stored gunpowder and other weapons here, for use in sieges or potential attacks against the French mainland."

"That's more like it!" Harry growled. "About

time we got to the part about besting the horrid French."

"Those same horrid French who gave us a spectacularly successful recording contract?" Emily reminded him, hands on hips.

"Even though we were just out of uni and hadn't the foggiest clue what on earth we were doing?" Marina added. The French music label, specialising in string repertoire and young quartets, had given them a tremendous boost and the opportunity to record some much-loved treasures.

"The very same," Harry continued. "Enemies of our blood, they are." He stood tall, like a Beefeater at the Tower of London, his dwindling coffee aloft in salute, bringing a good laugh from the others.

"That's the thing about you, Harry," Leo commented. "You know full well that you make absolutely no sense, and you just don't *care*."

"Nope," he replied. "I've got Union Jack underpants on. That's how I feel about the *French*."

Shaking their heads in unison, Emily and Marina moved on to the next exhibit about a traitor who was locked up in the dungeons for a dozen years, despite a marked paucity of evidence against him. "Well, at least he wasn't sentenced to death," Emily observed.

Marina peered into the tiny cell and imagined

for an uncomfortable second the life of someone incarcerated there year after year. "I don't know which I'd prefer," she admitted. "Might be better to get it over with quickly. Being stuck down here," she said, pausing to shiver slightly at the prospect, "would be my worst nightmare."

CHAPTER FOUR

THE AMBULANCE CREW checked for signs of life. Finding none and given the extent of the fallen man's injuries and the twenty-five minutes since the discovery of the body, no attempt was made to revive him. "We'll only complicate things for the post-mortem," the paramedic explained. "Tomlinson on his way, is he?"

The elderly pathologist arrived minutes later, partly winded after the long walk from the visitors entrance. "Inspector," he wheezed in greeting, loosening the top button of his shirt. He glanced at the body covered in stained white linen, the small crowd of wedding guests and staff keeping a respectful distance, curious and horrified by turns.

"And I'd hoped you were joking. That it might have been an exercise or something."

"Afraid not, Marcus. Found him myself. The wife was here, kneeling over him, but she did a runner." He was on the phone with Janice again. "I've got Barnwell and Roach looking for her."

"Ah, the dynamic duo," Tomlinson said. "We need have no fear, then," he quipped. Graham let him have his little joke and escorted him to the body.

Tomlinson checked the victim's pupils, took notes on the skin tone, and assessed the position of the body and its location. "Well, we can't rule out anything at this stage," Tomlinson began, "but these injuries look entirely consistent with a fall from a great height. Beyond that, I'll need to get in there and take a look."

Tomlinson's idiosyncratic style was a result of his many decades of experience. He was beyond shock and grief. He'd seen death in many forms, whether arrived at by accident, misadventure, despair, or through violence.

The pathologist made arrangements with the ambulance crew to have the body transported to the local hospital where he would carry out his post mortem. "What's your gut telling you, Marcus?" Graham asked.

"I don't believe in speculating about something

as serious as this," Tomlinson replied, a little haughtily. "But off the record, I wouldn't be surprised if something fishy went on here." He polished his glasses with his handkerchief and seemed unwilling to elaborate.

"Oh?" Graham prompted, ever hopeful that the elderly man might dispense more of his hard-earned wisdom.

"Well... How many men choose to end it all the day after getting married?" Tomlinson wondered aloud. "Most chaps wait eight or ten years." When Graham didn't respond to his black humour, Tomlinson continued. "And most suicides have empty pockets. Did you know that?"

"I think I did," Graham replied.

"This chap brought his driver's license with him. Very unusual in cases where there's no foul play."

They glanced up together at the looming battlements. "Hell of a fall," Graham commented. "He'd have needed to be *absolutely resolved*. You can imagine someone with suicidal thoughts getting up there, distracted by this amazing view of the Channel, and then looking over the edge and thinking..."

"'Sod this, I'm going to go slit my wrists instead,'" Tomlinson said. "It takes real guts to throw yourself from a high place."

Graham rubbed his chin thoughtfully. "I do wish the wife hadn't done a runner."

"Now why would she do a thing like that?" Tomlinson asked. It was a rhetorical question.

Graham walked the pathologist to the two waiting medics who were ready to depart with the man's body. "Thanks, Marcus. Stay in touch, okay?"

"I have a feeling, old boy, that I'm going to *have* to."

Graham took a seat in the castle's reception area, just a row of chairs beneath the huge arch of the main gate, and made a point of taking some deep breaths. Short of a cup of tea, something that he'd been without for far too long, a quiet moment to calm the senses and oxygenate his lungs was a sure-fire method of invigorating his deductive abilities. Frustratingly, though, his interviews with the staff and guests had so far revealed little more than he already knew. No one had seen a *thing*. Few were even awake at such an early hour, certainly not after the excesses of the evening before. The two witnesses who had come forward claimed to have heard the scream and only then come running just like he had.

Janice Harding arrived looking slightly flustered but with her uniform characteristically neat. "Sorry, sir. Car wouldn't start, would it? On this, of all mornings!"

"Morning, Sergeant." Graham smiled a little distractedly. He bid her sit down.

"You know, sir, I don't want to say the wrong thing or speak out of turn but..."

"There have been two mysterious deaths," Graham interjected, "within six weeks of each other," he added, "and both immediately following *my arrival* in Gorey."

Janice was a little red-faced to have it pointed out so bluntly. "Er, yes, sir."

"Am I a suspect, Sergeant?" he asked, turning to her with a weary look.

"No, sir!" she exclaimed. "I just meant..."

"Then let's leave coincidences and what-ifs to the conspiracy nuts and perhaps engage in some *police work*," he said, a little pointedly.

"Sorry, sir."

"It's okay, Janice. I was just looking forward to a peaceful Sunday under blue skies, and now I'm going to be interviewing distraught, teary relatives and listening to Tomlinson go on about compound hip fractures and intracranial haemorrhage. Come on, let's go. I fancy taking in the view from the top."

They made their way up to the top of the castle via a narrow, very steep, spiral staircase.

"I wouldn't fancy going up these in the shoes I was wearing last night, sir."

"This castle dates back to the 13th century. I don't think they envisaged Jimmy Choos back then, Janice. Probably didn't figure in the architect's plans."

Janice couldn't decide whether to chuckle at Graham's dry humour or be astounded that he knew what Jimmy Choos were. "I can assure you, sir, that my wages don't stretch to buying such fine, luxury items, but if you're willing to rectify that, I'm willing to accept your generosity.... Ah, here we are. Phew."

It was still chilly as they emerged into the sunlight, the brisk fresh air a welcome respite from the dustiness of the castle stairwell. Graham and Harding walked along the battlements and caught their breath.

"He fell," Graham said simply. "That's all we know."

"Falls," Harding explained, mostly to refresh her memory, "tend to fall, if you'll pardon the pun, into three categories according to the textbooks. There are accidents, for one."

"The battlements are secure, with good footing,

and it didn't rain last night," Graham intoned. "Maybe he was drunk."

"You'd need to have the worst possible luck to end up pitching over these walls. They're nearly five feet high and two feet deep," Harding added. "Unless this was a category two fall, and the victim was *pushed* over one of these window-thingies."

Graham smiled. "They're called crenellations. Soldiers defended themselves between these gaps. They might have shot arrows, poured scalding water through them, or taken advantage of the extra height to simply bludgeon their attackers from above."

They walked on some more, admiring the view. "We can't prove anyone else was up here. There are no surveillance cameras," Graham said, looking around, "and no witnesses report being here or hearing anything."

"Which leaves us with the third category, sir: suicide."

"Hmm."

CHAPTER FIVE

JANICE AND GRAHAM walked back down the ramparts to the castle's administrative area located next to the maze. In the quadrangle, the marquee assembled for the wedding the day before had already been struck down, leaving the square fetchingly green and open. In his office, Stephen Jeffries was at his desk staring out of the window. He jumped slightly as Graham knocked at the door.

"You startled me," Jeffries said, his hand flying to his neck. He collected himself. "Please, won't you sit down?"

"Mr. Jeffries, this is Sergeant Harding. She will be assisting me in this investigation."

Jeffries looked horrified. *"Investigation?"* he breathed. "So you think..."

Graham raised a hand. "Let's not jump to any conclusions," he said, grimacing inwardly at the unfortunate turn of phrase. "We are trained to observe the facts and then allow the prevailing circumstances to tell us what the body cannot."

At Harding's urging, Jeffries described in detail the events of the wedding, right down to the canapés and the music. "Everyone seemed happy. There were no arguments... except, well..."

"Except?" Harding prompted.

"I'm sure it was nothing, but the mother of the bride did give one of my staff a chewing out about the tiniest thing: the arrangement of the wine glasses. She wanted them laid out in a particular pattern... you know how mothers of the bride can be."

Janice let her gaze fall on her empty ring finger. "Not really. Did she speak much with the groom?"

"No more or less than normal," Jeffries replied. "I've attended a hundred weddings in one capacity or other, and it's surprisingly common for the two sides of the aisle to keep almost to themselves, certainly until the ceremony is over. It's later, when everyone's had enough alcohol that the barriers tend to crumble. That's usually when the bridesmaids find themselves in an unfamiliar bed or the groomsmen decide that streaking through Gorey in the small hours is simply the *best* idea they've ever had."

Graham made a note in his book: *booze.* They hadn't discounted a drunken mishap as the cause of George Ross's unfortunate demise. It would hardly be the first time a young man had drunk himself into a stupor and met with a grievous injury in the hours after his wedding.

"Well, Mr. Jeffries, we're keen not to disrupt things here at the castle, but we do need to interview a good number of the guests," Graham explained.

"Background information, mostly," Janice clarified. "Building a picture of the relationships, the tensions, you know. A bit of history."

Jeffries shook his head. "Oh, there's not a lot going on today, and I've already done my best to preserve things as they were. We'll close the gates to visitors, of course. Someone should already have done that. The construction crews have Sunday off and there are no other functions planned."

"Construction?" Harding asked.

"Yes, just some shoring up in the lower levels. This place needs constant maintenance, as you might imagine. I made sure they stopped drilling and hammering before the guests arrived yesterday, otherwise, we wouldn't have been able to hear the 'I dos,'" he smiled.

"Could you supply us with a copy of the guest list, annotated with room numbers, please. And we'll need to speak with your night security guard if he's still here."

"*She*," Jeffries pointed out, "is waiting in the Great Hall. I told Sam she might be needed, so she stayed on a little longer than usual."

Jeffries led Harding and Graham to the Great Hall, a giant space with a dozen long, ancient tables, six on each side, spaced out perfectly for lavish feasting. Another, even larger table sat at the head of the room. The tables had only been partially cleared and tablecloths, glasses, and the odd napkin still awaited removal. Graham noticed a stocky blonde woman in a dark blue uniform standing in the corner. She was obviously waiting for them. "Terrible, isn't it?" she said, shaking both their hands. "I'm Sam. Night security."

"It is, Sam. Tragic," Graham agreed. "Why don't you tell us what you saw?"

Sam shrugged. *Not a great sign*, Graham thought. "The wedding went off without a hitch. Lots of drinking, partying, dancing, the usual. People filtered away by about midnight. The couple was already gone by then, you know," she said with a slight smile, which vanished as she remembered that half of that same happy couple was now on a mortuary slab. "There was one drunken woman who stayed to the end, dancing by herself, until the DJ left at about two."

"Any disturbances?" Harding asked. "Fights? Arguments? Drunken brawls?"

"Oh, no," Sam reported. "Drunken brawls are my speciality, and there wasn't even a sniff of one."

Graham found himself smiling at the unswerving honesty of this straightforward character. "And what about this morning? At the time of the victim's fall?"

Another shrug. *Come on, Sam... Help us out here.*

"There was nothing untoward. No one was about."

Harding interjected. "There was a scream, the arrival of an ambulance, a crowd of people... Where were you during all of this?" she asked.

"Yes. I don't remember seeing you at all," Graham added.

Sam didn't shrug this time. Instead, she gave a resigned sigh. "Asleep," she admitted. "I'm on a new medication, you know, for my mood. Makes me sleepy sometimes."

"Where?" Graham asked, making a note in his ever-present notebook. "Where did you sleep?"

"I was crashed out on the couch in Mr. Jeffries'

office." She gave them both a worried glance. "You won't *tell* him, will you?"

"Mum's the word," Harding promised before Graham could say anything. She knew a genuine soul when she saw one.

"Thanks," Sam said, her shyness rather affecting after the brawny bravado of earlier. "Wish I could help more."

So do I. You have no idea how much. "You've been very helpful. Maybe get yourself home for some rest," Graham suggested, snapping his notebook shut.

CHAPTER SIX

THE GREAT HALL was among the rooms sealed off by Jeffries in his efficient zeal to preserve the record of the previous evening's events lest they shed some light on the case. Jeffries returned now to check whether he'd done the right thing.

"Few would have been so thoughtful, Mr. Jeffries," Graham told him, impressed for once. "You say that no one has been through here since the end of the dinner?"

"We have a policy," he said, "of letting our staff get themselves home at eleven. The bus service stops and cabs are a nightmare in Gorey on a Saturday night, as you might imagine. Instead," he explained, gesturing to the table linen and glassware, "we clean up during a 'blitz,' we call it, the next morning. Everyone comes in for three hours. We put on some music, I make big pots of coffee, and we get it all done."

"And this morning?' Graham asked, walking toward the top table.

"As soon as... Well, as soon as *it* happened, I called around and told them they weren't needed. If necessary, I'll clean up myself. Won't be the first time I've had these hands in hot water," he joked. "But I knew it'd be easier for you to work with fewer people here. Having twenty kitchen staff running about... Well, it didn't seem right under the circumstances."

Harding made notes. "You did the right thing, Mr. Jeffries. We're very grateful."

Graham was already at the top table, where plates seemed to have been left undisturbed since the previous evening. "This was George's place?" he asked. Jeffries nodded. "Would you be good enough to grab me a new box of zippered bags from the kitchen?" he added. "And a new pair of rubber gloves?"

Jeffries followed the request, and Graham began bagging up the dessert plate, silverware, and both the water and wine glasses from George's plate setting.

Harding was by his shoulder. "Poison?" she asked quietly. "Not poison, *again*?" In her head, she had the image of George, crippled by stomach pain and wracked by confusion, tottering over the battlements to his death.

A recent local headline-making investigation, only six weeks earlier, had poison at its crux, but Graham was in no mood to infer anything before gathering all the facts. "Let's see. I'm hoping to hear from Tomlinson soon. He might be able to tell us." Then, turning to the events manager, "Mr. Jeffries, could we bother you to show us the bridal suite?"

It was a room fit for a President or a King. Or, perhaps, a newlywed couple with deep pockets. Huge, and with a breathtaking view of the Channel and the French coast beyond, the bridal suite was beautifully appointed, complete with a four-poster canopy bed and all the finery a young couple in love could dream of.

"Not bad," Harding allowed. "What kind of, erm, cost are we talking, per night?" she asked, bracing herself for an answer bordering on the insane.

"About two thousand," Jeffries answered offhandedly as if asked the question by virtually everyone who visited the suite, which, of course, he was. "Depends on the time of year."

Harding suppressed a whistle of amazement and began taking in the details of the room. By her side, Inspector Graham was doing the same, but in that extraordinarily thorough way that he had made his own. She watched him absorbing the details, his eyes smoothly moving between each object, to the floor and across to the curtains, up to the ceiling, and then down to the bed. Graham's ability to gather, store, and analyse visual data was a finely honed mechanism. It was something of a thrill for Harding to watch these remarkable skills being exploited at full tilt.

"Notice anything, Sergeant Harding?" Graham opened up his notebook to write down what he had observed.

"Well..." She looked around more closely. "It appears to be a bridal suite, laid out beautifully, awaiting the happy couple." Then she stopped. "But... They were supposed to have been here hours ago... Before midnight, Sam said."

"Precisely," Graham agreed.

"The bed is still perfectly made... I mean, what couple..."

"Even bothers to properly make their own bed at home, let alone in a hotel where you're paying a month's wages to stay for one night?" Graham discounted the notion. "They didn't sleep here, Harding. They didn't touch the champagne." He gingerly lifted the bottle from a cold pool of melted ice in a bucket. "They didn't even nibble so much as a chocolate-covered strawberry, for heaven's sake."

"Weird," Harding almost whispered.

"I was married once," Graham said. "And immediately after the wedding reception, I had three things in mind." He ticked them off his fingers. "Food, because I'd barely eaten a thing amidst all the socialising and well-wishing. A glass of something strong, because I'd been too scared to drink in case I overdid it. And... well, bed. I was exhausted."

Harding blushed at this uncharacteristic outpouring of personal information, something that Jeffries caught, responding with the faintest of smiles. "I think most married couples have those same priorities, sir."

"Although not always in the same order," Jeffries added. "But what does it tell you about the couple that they didn't even come back here?"

"Or open their luggage?" Harding said next, opening the walk-in closet to reveal two suitcases.

Graham once more shut his notebook. Even after weeks of teasing by his two constables, he had resolutely refused to begin using a tablet. He found the leather-bound volume reassuring, a bulwark against the tides of constant change. "I really don't know, Mr. Jeffries," Graham admitted. "But it tells us *something*. I guarantee you that."

CHAPTER SEVEN

THE SIGN STATED, in terms not uncertain, *"EXHIBIT UNDER PREPARATION. NO ADMITTANCE."* But to Leo Turner-Price, this was a challenge, not an order. "Seems like an invitation to me."

"What does?" Emily asked, eyeing the sign. "They're working on that part, Leo," she said, as though to an errant seven-year-old who just *had* to see *everything*. "Let's head back up. I want to see the Great Hall."

Leo was unmoved. "You don't want to see what exhibit they're *preparing?*" he asked. "That doesn't pique your curiosity?"

"Nope," Emily replied.

"Mind's kinda piqued," Marina admitted.

"Why?" Harry asked. "I mean, it'll just be another preserved jail cell or something, right?" If the truth were told, he was enjoying the cool, dark surroundings. They were giving him welcome relief from the effects of last night's alcohol.

"Just a little look, and then we'll head up and see the Great Hall," Leo promised. "I want to see it too. I just want to see this first."

"Oh, for heaven's sake," Emily sighed, admitting defeat. She helped Leo shift the sign aside and slide back the bolt on the heavy wooden door. It opened with a long, deeply ominous creak. "Okay, now even *I'm* kinda curious," she admitted.

The room was dark, but there was a light switch on the wall by the door, just sufficiently illuminated by the bulbs that lit the main passageway. Leo flicked the switch and a single bare ceiling bulb came on. "Looks like they're still working on the lighting too." He peered into the gloom "Oh... No *way*..."

"Wait a minute, isn't that a..."

"Yep... I believe it is..."

A six-foot-tall iron maiden, a human-sized metal cabinet offering perhaps the least comfortable method of incarceration, stood open by the wall, spikes protruding from every angle. Beside that was a worryingly authentic-looking rack, complete with a naked mannequin who seemed doomed to suffer painful stretching for all eternity. In the corner was a set of wooden shelves that held torture instruments of every description. "Oh man, they need to get this opened up *straight away*. The museum would be *way cooler* if all this were on display," Leo declared.

It warmed Emily's heart that such an esteemed and much-cited historian was reduced to childish glee at the sight of a few old torture methods, and it stirred in her the affection she'd felt for this complex, clever man since their undergraduate days. She'd been quietly furious with him for threatening the integrity of the quartet by disappearing as he had for four long months after Marina had rejected him and was much relieved when he made contact once more. His reappearance had been tentative, much like a badger emerging from his sett, but the warm welcome he received from the group had been so joyous that the awkwardness of the situation was thankfully soon confined to the past.

Leo was examining a tapestry that adorned the far wall. It was perhaps sixteen feet square and extremely dusty, but he could make out a stylised battle scene of some sort, with horses in formation, their riders carrying pikes and swords. He lifted the material to examine it and found that the tapestry had been placed to neatly cover a small, wooden door.

"Hey..." Leo began. "There's another doorway here." He held up the dusty tapestry to show the others.

"What's this one marked? *Verboten?*" Marina quipped.

"*Private,*" Leo replied. "I mean, *private* to whom?"

Harry took a look. "I don't know. Maybe the people who run this place?" he posed. "Come on, buddy. You've had your fun. Let's get out of here before we're deported from Jersey for trespass under some 16th century law."

"Yeah," Emily joked, "they could imprison us down here or something. To discourage others."

Leo made a rude, dismissive noise, grinned at the other three, and opened the door with his shoulder. It took three firm shoves. "Gotcha!" he exclaimed.

"Er, Leo," Harry began, "don't you think, maybe if the door's been closed for so long that it needs a shoulder barge to open it, they might be serious about it being 'private?'"

Another rude noise and then Leo was gone, headed down whatever passage he had discovered. A few seconds later, "Oh... This is *so cool!*"

The others exchanged worried glances, but after three simultaneous shrugs, they followed Leo through the small wooden door and into a tunnel barely broad enough for two people to stand side-by-side. "Wow, Leo, what the heck have you found this time?" Marina asked.

"Must be a servant's tunnel or something," Leo responded, pleased to see that his friends had joined him.

"Leading from the castle's torture chamber?" Harry responded. "'Hither, servant, and heed my will. All this stretching and maiming and removal of teeth with a spoon has left me parched. Pray thee fetch a flagon of ale to quench mine raging thirst.' That kind of servant?"

Their laughter echoed down the tunnel. There was just enough light from the torture chamber for them to see that the passage opened up into a larger room, but beyond that, they could not see anything.

"Anyone else think this might be a good point to turn back?" Emily asked the group.

"No fatalities yet," Leo objected. "I say we see if there's a light switch in the next room."

Marina squeezed in beside him and gave him a friendly push forward. "I don't think they had light switches in the 1500s, genius."

Emily felt the skin on her neck begin to crawl unpleasantly. "You know, guys, I really don't think we should..."

A sharp sound behind them brought the group

to an abrupt halt. It was the sound of stone on stone, a collision of some kind.

"Okay, you're right. Let's do an about-face," Leo began, but there was another, more gradual sound, like stone sliding over something, and then a tumbling noise that boomed down the tunnel, bringing with it a cloud of dust and masonry before all the lights went out.

CHAPTER EIGHT

JEFFRIES DECIDED TO effectively hand over his offices in the administrative wing to the police. He felt it his duty to assist the investigation however he could, he was determined that the police discover what happened, and he was particularly anxious that the castle not suffer unduly from this unfortunate incident. If George Ross's death were a suicide, that would be something most people might accept without question, even that of a young man at the very outset of his married life. But something more suspicious, a *murder...*

The events manager couldn't help thinking back to the mutterings and rumours he'd heard about poor Mrs. Taylor and the White House Inn after that terrible business with the dead woman on the beach. Mrs. Taylor seemed to have recovered now, and a quick chat in the street the other day had revealed that bookings were strong—they were "getting on with it," as the redoubtable lady put it—but Jeffries was horrified at the notion of Orgueil becoming some kind of sensationalised "murder castle."

It was hard enough for him to market the place as a wedding venue, for all its virtues of facilities and location, when torture and illegal imprisonment had taken place in the castle's bowels. The delays to opening the torture exhibit were supposedly related to the construction work, but in reality, some among the museum's board still found the whole idea rather distasteful and had repeatedly asked for more time to mull over its implications.

Jeffries huffed a big sigh and turned his head as Detective Inspector Graham received the much-anticipated call from Marcus Tomlinson. "Hi, Marcus? Alright, lay it on me. Graham listened for a long moment taking notes. "You're quite sure?" He listened again, frowned at Harding, took more notes, thanked the pathologist, and ended the call.

"Damn," Graham muttered. "Not a lot to go on, I'm afraid." Harding looked crestfallen. Jeffries felt the same way.

"Tox screen?" Janice asked.

"Alcohol, but nothing out of the ordinary, especially for a man who'd got married the day before. No drugs, no painkillers, none of the usual set of poisons. He even checked for that unusual one we ran into six weeks back: no dice."

"So what do you think, sir? Could it be suicide?"

Jeffries shook his head. "I can't understand why someone would do that," he muttered darkly. "Such a terrible crime against those you leave behind."

"If he chose to end his life, he did it whilst all his closest family and friends were right here. Surely, if he had dark thoughts, he would have reached out to someone. His family, his best man... his new *wife*, for heaven's sake." Graham was incredulous.

"For me," Jeffries posited with the shyness of someone who felt they might be speaking out of turn, "it's a conundrum to consider that this man, who had just married Marie, a beautiful young woman from a loving family and," he added with a hint of pride, "in a *stunning* location, with great music and food.... that such a man could consider this the very *lowest point* of his life? Such an act is simply *inconceivable*," he said, his voice rising, his words now clear.

Graham was nodding and making more notes.

"Good points, Mr. Jeffries. Unless, of course, there are things we don't know. And there's nothing more certain than that." He turned to Harding. "Where do you think we should begin, Sergeant?"

Janice grabbed the list of wedding guests and scanned it. "Mr. Jeffries, am I seeing this right? The bride's parents did not stay at the castle last night?"

The events manager thought back for a second. "Oh, no. They didn't want to be among all the noise and partying after what I remember the bride's mother calling 'a challenging day.' Honestly, I didn't care for her at all. But, clients are clients, and we must..."

"Where?" Harding asked, without apologising for the interruption. Jeffries snapped his mouth shut as though he'd been rapped on the knuckles.

"At the White House Inn, of course."

Janice chose to make use of their unmarked police car for the visit to the White House Inn. Poor Mrs. Taylor had seen more than enough uniformed men and women come and go during their investigation the previous month, and neither Harding nor Graham wanted to bring back bad memories. Not only had the inn owner been a stalwart help during the murder inquiry, but she had also extended

Graham every courtesy since. The least they could do was keep her lobby free of further intrigue and unpleasantness.

"Oh, Sergeant Harding!" Marjorie Taylor exclaimed happily, her necklace of giant beads bouncing. "Good to see you. Are you staying for lunch with the Detective Inspector?"

Graham quieted her with a serious look and cast a glance at the back office. They walked over to it and closed the door. "I want to do this discreetly, Mrs. Taylor," Graham said. "You're going to be hearing about a sudden and mysterious death at the castle."

Mrs. Taylor's hands flew to her mouth. "Not again!" she gasped.

"The groom from a big wedding last night took a tumble from the battlements," Graham added, finding that his attempt to soften the tragedy had been a near-miss at best.

"Oh no!" Mrs. Taylor cried. She swayed as though about to pitch onto the traditionally patterned carpet of ferns and flowers beneath her.

"Steady, love, steady," Harding cooed, her hand on the older woman's shoulder. "Very quietly, we need to have a word with Mr. and Mrs. Joubert, parents of the bride. We understand they stayed with you last night."

Mrs. Taylor searched her memory, glad of the

distraction. "Joubert? Yes... They might be at break-fast." A brief check and a glance at the dining room proved Mrs. Taylor correct. A couple in their fifties were eating a leisurely breakfast by the window.

"Let's wait until they're finished, eh? We'll knock on the door of their room when they return," Graham said.

Graham and Harding tried to blend in with the guests filtering through the reception area. There were some new arrivals, others checking out, families heading out for the day, and couples wandering through, hand in hand. "Nice and normal," Harding observed. "Best this way."

"Hmm?" Graham asked.

"That we don't make a big splash, you know."

Graham spotted the Jouberts making their way up to their room and checked his watch. "You're learning one of the most important lessons of police work," he told Janice. "Never cause a big fuss if you don't have to."

A few minutes later, rather nervous but reassured to have the experienced Graham alongside her, Harding knocked on the Joubert's door. "Breathe, Sergeant," he advised. "I can do the talking if you'd prefer."

"I've got this," she told him, though her shaking hand told Graham otherwise. Janice had only done one other "notification of death," and that had been to the granddaughter of an old man who had been hit by a car. The young woman had taken it mercifully well, but Harding had to wonder if notifying the Jouberts of the death of their brand new son-in-law would be a tougher experience.

CHAPTER NINE

"**M**ADAME MATHILDE ET *Monsieur Antoine Joubert?*" Sergeant Harding asked in her best French accent. Confirming their names wasn't simply courtesy. Every notification required the identification of the family.

"*Oui*," Antoine Joubert replied, a crease of concern appearing between his eyebrows.

"May we come in for a moment, please, sir?" Harding asked. All four of them stood in the spacious hotel room whilst Sergeant Harding delivered the terrible news.

Neither took it well. Antoine Joubert was a tall, haughty, restaurateur, the owner of a bistro in St. Malo. Joubert clutched a fist to his forehead and began to pace, muttering in French under his breath. He was not unused to tragedy, but he was devoted to his family and clearly horrified at the news.

Mathilde, his short, stocky wife, was equally affected. When she heard the news, she went as pale as her bed linen. *"Mais... C'est incroyable!"* she cried for the third time as she was helped to a chair by Janice.

Graham prided himself on his ability to recognise genuine shock from the artificial, theatrical kind, and all the signs were that the Jouberts were exhibiting the real thing. Unless he was quite wrong, they did not know of George's death or their daughter's strange and confusing disappearance.

"We have no reason to believe that George's death was anything other than an accident, but it is, as I'm sure you'll agree, especially ill-timed."

"But it is hours..." *Monsieur* Joubert was stuttering, badly shaken, "only *hours* after his marriage to my daughter. How can this have happened?" He went to sit in a chair next to his wife who now sat in a daze. "How?" he repeated, tending to her by tenderly wiping her face with a handkerchief.

"That's what we intend to find out," Harding told him. "Our first step is to interview anyone who might have seen the... accident, or perhaps heard conversations between George and someone else."

Mathilde Joubert raised teary eyes to look at Harding. "Arguments? On his wedding day? *Impossible...*" she muttered. She began to cry with a long, moaning sob.

"What about Marie? Has she been told? Is she alright?" Antoine was anxious about his daughter.

"Your daughter ran off after her husband's fall. She left him lying on the ground."

This news exhibited another wail from *Madame* Joubert.

"So," Graham insisted, "We must speak with everyone. I'm sorry to do this so soon after you've received the news but can you tell us about the wedding?"

Mathilde was breathless as she recovered from her wailing, so Antoine took over. "It was elegant, beautiful," he reported. "Everyone had a wonderful time." He was distant for a moment, perhaps thinking back to the previous day's highlights. "Wonderful," he repeated. "No arguments or bad feelings. Just a happy couple, two delighted families. Lots of dancing, drinking. You know how it is."

"Of course," Graham said, making his usual notes. "How late did you stay at the festivities?"

Antoine thought for a second. "Perhaps eleven or a little after. We were both tired, my wife especially. We're not used to big parties at our age."

"And you returned directly here, to the White House Inn?" Harding confirmed.

"Yes. We were asleep within moments. It had been a very long day," Antoine replied.

Graham took the unusual step of sitting on the edge of the bed, a couple of feet from the grieving couple. Harding watched him work, curious as ever, but confident that this experienced and brilliant detective could glean whatever evidence was required.

"*Monsieur*," Graham began, his voice deliberately low, "could you think of anywhere Marie might have run to at this terrible time? Perhaps somewhere on Jersey?"

His arm around his crying wife, Antoine shook his head. "They had plans for a honeymoon. I don't know where. They refused to tell us, you know... it was a couple's secret."

Graham nodded. His own, modest honeymoon had been a confidence mercifully well kept. School friends of his were less fortunate. They had arrived at their secluded honeymooners' cottage to find six chickens in the kitchen and the phone disconnected. "Is there anywhere else she might have chosen to go?"

"St. Malo?" Mathilde suggested.

"*Non, chérie*," Antoine said. "The boat doesn't leave for another hour or two. And the flights are always full. I can't see how she can have gone home." Then he added, "And I can't see *why* she would."

Harding asked the next question. "Where was the couple staying before the wedding? I understand they drove separately to the castle. Marie in a Rolls Royce?"

The French couple nodded. "I arranged a little place just outside Gorey," Antoine told them, "on the hill overlooking the beach. A nice place for a bride to quietly prepare for her big day." Antoine reached into his wallet for the address. "George had an apartment. Marie would stay there with him but for the wedding, she went to this place. So he not see her as is the custom."

"Is there anything more you can tell us? Any small detail?"

Antoine stood. "Sir... I hope this is not the conclusion you are forced to draw," he said severely, "but if... if this were *murder*... I want to know, *at once*, who was responsible."

Graham drew himself up to the older Frenchman, they were about the same height. "*Monsieur* Joubert, it's important not to jump to any..."

"George was my family. He joined us not once but twice. And my family are the dearest thing to me in the world."

Harding and Graham exchanged confused

glances. "Forgive me, *Monsieur* Joubert," Graham said. "Did you say, 'twice?'"

Mathilde reached out to her husband as if to stop him. "Antoine... *S'il vous plait...*"

Her husband patted her hand but pushed on. "My wife is not well," he explained. "This has been the most terrible shock." Then he addressed Harding. "I recognise it is a little unusual, but George has had the honour of marrying first one and then the other of my beautiful daughters."

Harding's face remained impassive, despite the overwhelming impulse to raise both eyebrows. She limited herself to a curious, "Is that so?"

"*Oui*," Antoine replied, clearly more accustomed than either Graham or Harding to the notion that a man might marry a woman before divorcing her and marrying her sister. "George and Juliette first. They had a baby, our granddaughter. She is in St. Malo with her stepfather, Juliette's new husband. But our Juliette is... how can I say...?" He searched the room's walls for the word. "*Flighty?*"

"I think I understand, sir," Graham replied, scribbling notes.

"Will she be able to help us, do you think?" Harding tried.

Antoine gave a short, hollow laugh. To Graham's ears, it was not the kind of noise any father should ever make about his daughter. It conjured up the idea that Juliette was an apple that had fallen very far from the family tree indeed.

"She has problems," Mathilde said simply, beginning to gather herself. "Drinking. Smoking things she should not. You understand." It wasn't a question, but a request to move on.

Harding thanked the couple, and Graham made his final notes before they left. "Rest assured, no stone shall remain unturned." Graham immediately doubted that the expression would translate well into French and so added, "We'll do our very best."

They left the Jouberts to their indisputable grief, closing the door quietly. "Well, Sergeant," the inspector said as they crossed the lobby and waved courteously to Mrs. Taylor, "what did you make of *that?*"

They reached the car and Harding sat in the driver's seat, thinking carefully. "I'd say, Detective Inspector, that if I ever married a fella, and then he left me and married my little sister, Christina," Janice's fists coiled as though strangling a snake, "I'd spend the rest of *my* life making *his* a bloody misery."

The two police officers sat in their unmarked car by the side of the road leading away from Gorey. The bright Sunday midmorning sunshine was making it difficult to see the phone's screen. "The wonders of modern technology," Graham breathed. "When on earth did you do this?"

"Soon as I got to the scene," Harding explained, "and started bagging up his effects. Routine, these days," Harding replied. "At police college, I remember them telling us over and over, 'Pictures, or it never happened.'"

Graham raised the phone again and turned it to get a better look at the picture of George Ross's driver's license. "I'd like to think that a notebook and pencil still count for something," Graham retorted.

"Only if you're a dinosaur. With respect, sir."

Graham shrugged off the remark. It was far from Harding's first at the expense of her boss and his stubborn refusal to be "upgraded," as she put it. "What works for me, works for me," he assured her.

"No arguing with that, sir," Harding said. "So, where should we start? Marie's rented cottage on the hill just over there," she said, pointing to the next rise, "or George's bachelor pad?"

Before Graham could answer, his phone rang. Resolute in his disregard for technology, the phone was a bulky, ancient model, barely capable of having an address book. Harding stifled a fit of giggles as Graham took the call.

"Ah, yes... Thank you so much for calling back." Graham listened and took notes, the chunky phone trapped between ear and shoulder. "What's that you say?" he asked, his face concerned. "Well... that's something, isn't it?" He listened on for three or four minutes, but all Harding could hear was a heavily-accented English, the words indistinguishable. "Right... Well, look, I can't thank you enough. Would you do me a favour and keep me informed if anything else comes up?" he asked.

The call ended and Graham completed another page of notes before turning to Harding. "That was my opposite number in St. Malo, erstwhile home of the Joubert clan. I put a call into them to do some delving into the family, see what they could tell us. And Poirot over there told me something rather interesting."

"Poirot was Belgian, sir."

Graham pushed on. "He claims that there is something of a murky background to this story."

"Oh?"

"The Ross family owned a farmhouse outside of St. Malo."

Graham laid out the narrative just as his French counterpart had related it. "It seems there was an incident back in the day involving both of George's parents. A murder-suicide."

This brought Harding to a standstill. "Good grief," she breathed.

"Although, it depends on whom you ask. Opinion is divided, even among the French police."

"So what happened?" Harding wanted to know.

"According to the official report, George's father shot his mother and then turned the gun on himself. George, who was thirteen at the time, and his sister Eleanor, eleven, were playing in a neighbouring field and came back to find them."

"Bloody hell," Harding exclaimed. "Can you imagine the effect that must have had on him?"

"Only slightly," Graham conceded. "But other relatives, including young George's paternal uncle and his maternal aunt, adamantly disputed that it was a murder-suicide. They claim that the family was entirely happy, loved being in France, and had even planned on moving there permanently after George and his sister had grown and left home."

"Hmm," Harding said, mulling this over. "Got to say, boss, it gives me a funny feeling."

Graham started the car. "Let us follow that funny feeling, Sergeant Harding. I suspect it might lead us in some very profitable directions."

CHAPTER TEN

AMIDST THE RUBBLE in the castle basement, the musical quartet crouched together. Surrounding them was that all-encompassing kind of darkness known only to those who explore the world's caves. Even in the hour since the tunnel's collapse, their eyes had not adjusted because there was simply no light to see by. The air was thick with dust. It had caused repeated coughing fits, but as it settled, the musicians resolved to stay still and wait for help as their breathing got easier. A stream of fresh air was coming from somewhere, but it was swelteringly hot.

"Okay, did we bring any water?" Emily said

after a gap in the discussion during which their prospects for survival dominated.

"I have this small bottle," Harry said, "I've drunk a third of it." It had been part of his anti-hangover plan.

"But basically, thank goodness, we're unhurt," Emily said next. "Basically, right?"

"'Basically' is right," Marina moaned. She had taken some kind of sharp, rocky impact which had left her shoulder and upper arm bruised and swollen. The others complained about the dust, but by some miracle, there were no serious injuries.

"Could have been a lot worse," Harry reminded them.

"It is what it is," Emily countered, quickly. "So, people, I want to get out of here immediately. Any thoughts?"

"Well," Leo said, "I think you'll agree that yelling didn't work."

Within moments of discovering that they still could, the group had screamed themselves hoarse in a long, continuous canon of all four voices but had heard absolutely nothing by way of a reply.

"Yeah, walls are too thick. Or maybe there's nobody in this part of the castle," Harry surmised. "We might have to dig our way out."

This too was a notion they'd visited before. "With what?" Marina asked. "We'd need shovels, picks, maybe even heavy lifting gear. We've only got four pairs of hands, and I don't know how much weight my shoulder will move. And I definitely don't want to do something that might bring the whole lot down on top of us."

Leo moved close to her—or, at least, over to where her voice was coming from. Marina made no move to stop him as he gently put a comforting arm around her. "I'll be careful of your shoulder," he promised in a whisper.

"Better had, or we'll be dealing with the aftermath of a fatality after all," she replied, only half-joking.

Emily held her phone aloft, something she'd done only sparingly since the crisis began, the better to spare its battery. "We've got four of these, right?"

Harry made a strangled, apologetic noise. "I left mine in my cello case."

"Three of these," Emily said, resolved to be accepting of whatever circumstances they found themselves in. Her priority was to focus on solving the problem of getting them out. "Anyone getting *any kind* of signal?"

In the dark, Leo shook his head. "Not a bloody thing. There's no reception, no internet, no local wireless."

Marina summed it up. "So, three highly sophisticated mobile communications devices capable of speaking with outer space and almost every human on earth just became three torches?"

Emily sighed. "That's about the size of it. But at least we have them. Let's keep their batteries for as long as we can." The torch functions of all three phones, supremely bright and useful as they were, drained the batteries at an alarming rate.

"Give me a quick bit of illumination over here," Harry said. "I think I've found a gap in the rockfall. It's not big, but if we can enlarge it, we might see where it leads..."

"Don't touch *anything*," Emily ordered. "Marina's right. If we disturb things, the ceiling might come crashing down."

"Look," he said, shining Marina's phone in the corner of the chamber they stood in. "Check it out."

The tunnel's collapse had obliterated the passage through which they had come. That end of the chamber now culminated in a tall pile of jagged rock and masonry that looked completely impassable. However, at the other end, where they'd seen, seconds before the collapse, that the tunnel opened up into a room of some kind, the pile of rocks was not quite as high. "Looks more like a possibility," Harry declared and reached to begin moving the debris.

"No!" Emily repeated more forcefully. "Don't touch the rocks."

"Look," Harry began. "I'll be really careful. If anyone hears anything moving around like it's going to fall, I'll stop."

Emily frowned in the darkness. "I still don't like it."

Leo weighed in. "You're first violin, Emily," he said, "not our Health and Safety officer. Let Harry have a try. It might be our only way out."

There was a long pause as Emily considered this. Finally, she acquiesced with audible reluctance. "Okay... Just go really, *really* slowly. We have no idea what else is in store."

Harry moved very deliberately. "I'll take the advice," he said, taking a small rock from the pile, "of the first man ever to make a spacewalk."

Marina heard this and couldn't resist, "What, 'always hit the bathroom before you go?'"

No one laughed, but they all appreciated her attempt. "He said, 'Think five times,'" Harry told the group, taking a firm grip on a larger rock and sliding it out of the pile, "'before moving a finger, and *ten times* before moving a hand.'"

Within moments, he had demonstrated that the rocks could be moved, apparently without disturbing anything fundamental.

Marina held her phone and provided light

whilst the other three carefully carried away rocks from the top of the blockage. They placed them at the opposite end of the mini-chamber in which they were trapped. The temperature began to fall as cooler air made its way through. "Doing better," Harry told them. He was closest to the jumble of rocks. "I can see how we might scramble over this stuff and into the next room."

"But what's in the next room?" Marina asked, half-rhetorically.

"It'll be better than in here. Not as hot, more air, more space. And maybe even another door, leading back to the main passageway," Emily speculated. "Wouldn't that be cool?" She'd taken on the role of morale booster and coach from the very outset. It would have been easy to simply give up and wait for help, but she was determined to keep the group positive and proactive in their search for a solution, even if she had had a slight wobble moments earlier. Even, she remained convinced, if the slightest mistake might bring the whole tunnel down on top of them.

CHAPTER ELEVEN

INSPECTOR GRAHAM STOOD in front of a three-story, white building which except for the local road and a small green on the edge of the cliff, looked directly onto the English Channel. Glancing over, Graham saw that the stretch of water was at its most spectacular, glittering blue in the midday sun.

He finished the rest of his water in a long gulp and pushed the intercom button for the second-floor apartment. He was not, in all honesty, expecting any kind of reply. Unless George and his fiancée had allowed guests to use their apartment for the weekend, there shouldn't be anyone inside. This expectation was shocked from him when a woman's voice called out. "Yes, who is it?"

"Detective Inspector Graham of Gorey Police, ma'am. Could I you open the door, please?"

"Police?" came the woman's voice.

"Just a routine inquiry. Would you mind if we spoke inside?"

There was a long pause—far longer than Graham was comfortable with. One of his least favourite ways to waste time was being left to hang around "like a lemon," as his mother used to say. It irritated him intensely when others dallied or did something they considered more important than keeping him waiting. There wasn't even a wisecrack from Harding to keep him occupied. She had gone on to check in with Barnwell and Roach who were conducting more interviews with the staff at the castle. Finally, there was a buzz and the door opened.

Graham climbed the stairs and found his way to the second floor flat with a bright red door. He knocked.

"Just a second..."

"It's rather urgent, ma'am. Part of a police inquiry," he said, raising his voice to make sure he'd be heard over the noise of the knocks and rumbles that the woman was making. It sounded as though she were cleaning the apartment.

"Hang on..."

Graham got that troubled, annoyed feeling that

he was being played. "Would you open the door, please?" he said, rather more loudly than before. Ten seconds later, as he was about to pound the door, it popped open as far as the chain would allow.

"Yes?" It was a woman in her late twenties. In that first fraction of a second when an investigative mind is at its most acute, Graham took in the details. There was a fatigue, a paleness, like that of someone whose last few hours had been difficult, even harrowing.

"Good afternoon," Graham began. "We're investigating the..." Then, after another second, it struck him. It was her. "Mrs. Ross?" he asked.

"Yes," she admitted.

The inspector's initial excitement was tempered by his training. "Is everything alright, ma'am?" he asked.

"*Must* you come in?" she said. "Bad day. With everything."

Graham blinked a few times. "Well, ma'am, with respect, it's the 'everything' that I'm here to talk to you about. Would you mind?" he said, gesturing to the chain on the door.

The woman sighed. "Come in, then," she said. She unhooked the chain and let him into the light, airy apartment.

Marie Ross placed herself on the couch and

then sighed again, this time so deeply that Graham thought she might simply vanish down into the cushions, never to be seen again. "I'm sad," she said without preamble. "Confused." There was a pause. "He was wonderful," she said simply. She turned to stare out the window.

"May I say how sorry we all are for the tragic events of this morning," Graham said. "Everyone I've spoken to assures me that George was very much loved and respected."

Marie was a beautiful woman, ephemeral almost. Her long, straight, dark hair hung loose and swished from side to side when she moved. Graham noticed her deep blue eyes were framed with long black lashes that gave her the look of an innocent child. He had to remind himself that she was possibly anything but.

He reached for his notebook, and though not invited, he sat on the smaller couch opposite Marie. Observing her, he noticed just how tired she looked. Perhaps it wasn't surprising given the circumstances, but he'd seen junkies with more life in their eyes. "Is there anything you'd like to tell me about what happened this morning?"

Marie peered as though seeing him for the first time. "Maybe. I'm not sure. I don't remember much."

"Mrs. Ross, I was there within moments of your

husband's fall. It was I who tried to help you both, just after it happened. Do you remember seeing me there? Asking you questions?"

The brand new wife and even newer widow seemed to search a very fragmented memory, her eyes darting around, and then said, "No. Not even a little bit. I hadn't thought anyone else was there."

Making notes on her demeanour, as well as everything she said, Graham continued, "Mrs. Ross, you left the scene in a considerable hurry. Before, in fact, it was certain that George was beyond help. May I ask why you did that?"

She screwed up her face in a strangely child-like way and thought hard. "You know," she said in a dreamy voice, "the first thing I remember after all the screaming and blood... was being back here." She glanced around. "Yes. I think I must have run all the way."

Graham thought this through, imagining the journey in his mind. "That's well over a mile, Mrs. Ross. You must have been exhausted."

"I went... Yes, I think I went straight to sleep when I got back. Like a... a kind of self-protective coma or something," she said haltingly. "I think I knew what had happened, but there was no way I could bring myself to think about it. I'm surprised," she added, "that I'm able to think about it now. But

I took some of the pills my doctor gave me, and I'm feeling a little better."

Graham scribbled. "May I see the bottle of pills, Mrs. Ross?"

Marie stood stiffly and winced, obviously aching all over. She fetched a bottle from her nightstand. "Anti-anxiety," she explained, handing Graham the transparent, orange container. "I take others too. Anti-depressives. Anti-psychotics. I asked my doctor," she related with a funny smile, "whether he had antiperspirants I could take, so I wouldn't have to remember to use my roll-on each morning, but he said I was being silly."

Graham looked at her for a long moment before taking down the prescription information along with the prescribing doctor's name and phone number. "What do you do for a living, ma'am?" he asked.

"Accounts firm," Marie said. "In St. Helier. Just for the last few months."

As he wrote the firm's name down, Graham privately questioned why *anyone* would be willing to entrust their financial matters to someone on so many drugs.

"Mrs. Ross, I have to ask... do you know of anyone who might have wanted to hurt your husband?"

She blinked again. "You know, I haven't got

used to calling him that yet. He was my fiancé and before that, my boyfriend. And before that," she paused slightly, "my brother-in-law." Again, she turned to look out the window.

Graham nodded. "I spoke with your parents a little while ago. Your father told me about the situation with Juliette, George, and yourself."

Marie Ross's mildly confused expression deepened. She appeared deeply puzzled, like a staggeringly drunk person trying to figure out why the pub vending machine failed to dispense the cigarettes they'd paid for. "Parents?" she said, almost experimentally. "*My* parents?"

Graham referred back to his notes. "Mathilde and Antoine Joubert. Your mother and father." Graham paused, concerned that some major mistake had been perpetrated and instantly wondering who was responsible. "No?"

"No," Marie replied, puzzling over this information. "No, I don't know who they are."

Graham persisted. "Mrs. Ross, they assured me that Juliette and you are their daughters. They were very upset at the whole…"

"No, that's wrong," Marie said, more confidently. "I was raised in foster homes in France. From the age of five. I've never had a permanent home. Never knew who my parents were."

"Your name *is* Marie Joubert? Recently married

to George Ross at Orgueil Castle?" Graham was bewildered.

"Oh yes," she said as if this information fit perfectly with what had come before.

Graham felt it best to stop there. Things had become too weird. Marie Ross wasn't making any sense. "Mrs. Ross, I'd like you to accompany me to our police station to help us with our inquiries," he said. "You're not under arrest, and you can refuse, but I think it'll be better for everyone that way."

Without a word, Marie gathered some things—her red leather handbag, a light jacket, and the bottle of pills Graham had been holding—and followed him from the apartment. He ushered Marie to the car, and then, having closed the door, called Harding.

"Janice? Do me a favour and bring the Joubert parents down to the station, would you? Yes, right away, if you can. We'll meet you there." Then, he thought it best to prepare her. "Something *bloody funny* is going on."

CHAPTER TWELVE

THE JOUBERTS STOOD stoically in the lobby of Gorey's tiny police station. Antoine was almost a foot taller than his wife, strong and wiry. They both walked toward the doors, ready to welcome their daughter as Graham approached with Marie in tow.

"*Chérie,*" they said in unison, but Marie simply stared at them. The Jouberts reached out to hug her, but she stepped aside. Twin streams of French followed, incomprehensible to both Graham and Harding who watched this strange reunion from the door of her office.

Marie said nothing, but she turned to Graham. "I don't know these people," she said. "I've never seen them before."

Horrified beyond measure, the Jouberts looked at each other, then to Marie, then to Inspector Graham. They did not speak. Harding assumed that they *could* not, that they were dumbfounded.

"*Monsieur* Joubert, *Madame* Joubert, are you prepared to swear that this is your daughter? Beyond any doubt whatsoever?" Graham said, hoping the formality of the request would jog some sense into their daughter.

"*Bien sur!* Of course!" They answered together. Then Antoine rounded on Graham. "How could you suspect that we might not know our own daughter? What ridiculous parents we would be!"

Marie stood silently amidst this confusion. She looked at one and then the other of this middle-aged French couple, without even the slightest recognition, as if they were two strangers brought in from the street. Harding looked on, completely baffled.

"Okay," Graham said. "Let's all take a seat and sort this out." He sounded more optimistic than he felt. This was more than something *bloody funny*. The investigation had taken a turn for the truly bizarre. "Marie, I'd like you to go with Sergeant Harding. She'll get you some coffee and maybe chat a bit. *Monsieur* and *Madame* Joubert, I'd like you to sit with me for a few minutes. I'm sure we'll straighten this out."

Harding took Marie to the furthest interview

room, whilst Graham took the closest. As he was settling the Jouberts in and trying to remember where the coffee was kept, the constabulary phone rang.

"Inspector Graham, Gorey Police," he said, hardly thrilled at the interruption and praying that it might shed some light on the conundrums he faced.

"Afternoon, sir," the young police officer said at the other end, stuttering slightly. He was always a little on edge when addressing his boss. "It's Constable Roach. We're at the castle."

Graham grabbed a notepad. "What's the latest, Constable?" *And try to keep it brief, for heaven's sake.* Roach had the habit of both repeating himself and wandering off topic when relaying information. Graham was training him to provide "just the facts."

Roach hoped to sound competent and efficient. "Well, we've just now finished interviewing the staff, like you asked, and I'm afraid there isn't much to report. Nobody seems to have seen anything amiss. Typical wedding, all the usual stuff. No one saw the fall."

"Makes sense," Graham said, half to himself.

"There's something else, sir."

"Oh?" Graham said, pencil at the ready.

"The castle management asked us to stay

around for a while, sir, and help with a separate matter."

Oh, hell's teeth. What now?

"Seems they managed to let in a group of visitors before the place was sealed off as a potential crime scene," Roach explained.

"So, have you escorted them out?" Graham asked pointedly, unsure as to why this trivial detail was suddenly important.

Roach cleared his throat. "We can't find them, sir. Looked everywhere."

Graham sighed. "People don't just vanish, Constable," he reminded his younger colleague. "How many are we talking?"

"A group of four. The receptionist says she recognised them as the musicians who played at the wedding yesterday. Came back for a look around the castle."

Graham shook his head. "Missing musicians. Just what we need. Look, get along and find them, will you? Let's just hope they've found the wine cellar and are having a fantastic time down there. And if they've buggered up my crime scene, we'll have words, Constable, you can be sure of that."

"Righto, sir. Over and out." The line clicked and Graham took three slow, deliberate breaths before heading to the interview room to sort out the mess that his case was becoming.

Deeply upset, muttering together in French, the Jouberts held hands and wished away this mysterious calamity. "We cannot understand," Antoine said, again and again. "Our daughter doesn't even *recognise* us."

His wife continued, "She has not been well. She has many problems. But her doctor is the best, and he insisted that she was... 'ow do you say... *stable*. Not a danger. Getting better, maybe."

"Yes, getting better," Antoine assured Graham.

Graham could see that there was little to be gained from speculating upon how it was that Marie was suddenly a stranger to her own family. "I'd like to talk about George," Graham said. "Once my colleague, Sergeant Harding, has interviewed Marie, perhaps we'll learn more about her state of mind. But for now, tell me some more about the man who was your son-in-law." *Two times over.*

The couple conferred for a moment in French. Graham didn't care for this one bit. He felt they might be colluding, or hiding something, or preparing to deliver some previously-concocted story. He cleared his throat.

Antoine took the lead. "George was... a very *limited* man, Inspector. Almost *simple*. Not sophisticated, not especially cultured in the ways of the world."

Graham made notes including one that Antoine was entirely unafraid, it seemed, to speak ill of the dead, even less than half a day after his son-in-law's demise.

"He was a teacher, you know. Not the best," Antoine continued. "He was very quiet. Spent too much time with his nose in a book, eh?"

Mathilde shrank a little more at each new insult, but she remained silent.

"He didn't know how to have fun. Was too … stiff? Like you British are." Antoine made a brief and absurd parody of some kind of wooden man, lumbering along a street. "No *joie de vivre*. No, not even a little. Just… *sad*," Antoine concluded, looking pointedly at Graham.

Graham ignored the affront to his fellow countrymen and perhaps himself and waited for more, but Antoine had run dry. "*C'est ça*," he concluded. *That's that.* "But my wife thinks very differently."

"Oh?" Graham said, turning to Mathilde. "Please… what can you tell me about your son-in-law, *Madame* Joubert?"

CHAPTER THIRTEEN

TIRED AND OVERWROUGHT by the day's extraordinary events and visibly unwilling to disagree with her husband but doing so anyway, Mathilde Joubert's delivery was halting and not simply because she was struggling to express herself in a second language.

"George Ross was the best thing that ever happened to our family," she explained. "The *best*. He was kind and gentle. He read big books, *littérature*, and he knew much about the world. He was a good husband to Juliette but she rejected him. She preferred the parties and the good times and... you know..." she screwed up her face in disgust and almost spat out the word, *"drugs."*

Graham's pencil never stopped moving. "I see."

"When she tired of him, she left to marry a no-body who simply had enough money to support her... excesses. I looked after George, made sure he was alright. He was broken-hearted by Juliette. Very ... how can I say...?"

"I think I understand," Graham offered.

"*Bien*. And so, Marie and I took care of him, helped him to find some work, new friends, places to go out. He was obsessed with the other man after Juliette left him. You know, he couldn't stop thinking about it. We helped him focus on some-thing else, something *good*."

Antoine chipped in. "This was when Marie and George became close." His fingertips drummed the tabletop. "Too close, for my preference."

Mathilde continued, her confidence building. "George was not the perfect man. But, neither is my husband. Neither are you, *Inspecteur*." Both men took her comments with good grace. Antoine gave a classically Gallic shrug. "He was an *héros*, too. We were proud of him." She looked sharply at her hus-band. "But you know this already, of course." Turning a page in his notebook, Graham confessed that he did not.

"Oh, it was in all the newspapers! It was a few years ago, his little moment of fame. When he was living in France with Juliette." Mathilde launched into the story whilst Antoine sat passively, entirely unimpressed. "He taught the young children, you know, at his school, but he also led some of those weekend *aventures*. When the children learn to camp and make fires and such. Yes?"

Graham nodded, writing constantly. "The Scouts?" he wondered aloud.

"Something like this. So, they were in the little boats... how do you say?" She mimed a paddling motion.

"Canoes?"

"*Ah, oui*. They were in *le port*, not far out at sea. Well, it should have been a safe place, but there was a sudden storm. Rain and wind and lightning. The children were all terrified. They were not experienced, you see."

"Sounds like a difficult situation," Graham said, inscribing reams of what looked like hieroglyphs, but which comprised a highly efficient, personalised, note-taking system.

"Three of the... little boats? The *canoes*?" Mathilde said, finding the word again. "Yes, three of them went over," she said, miming throughout. "The children were in the water. George tied the others together and then jumped into the sea to save them. Six young lives, *Inspecteur*. They would have died without him, for sure."

"Extraordinary," Graham agreed.

"*Mais oui*. He was very quiet about it. Didn't give any interviews or make a big noise. George knew family *tragédie* too well. Perhaps this was what made him so certain to save all their lives. Even risking his own."

"Tragedy?" Graham prompted.

"Yes, of course! George's parents," Mathilde began. "They..."

"Mathilde, *ce n'est pas important,*" Antoine instructed his wife.

Graham's French was, by his own admission, quite terrible, but this snippet was one he could fully understand. "*Monsieur* Joubert, I'd be glad if you'd allow *me* to decide the importance of these details." The surly restaurateur scowled briefly but made no argument "Carry on, please, *Madame* Joubert."

"George's parents died when he was thirteen. Maybe you know this," Mathilde said. "Terrible. The most *'orrible* accident."

Graham flicked back to his notes on the incident at the farmhouse. "I understand the police eventually ruled it to be a murder-suicide."

Antoine failed or chose not to censor the thought before it reached his mouth. "Maybe suicide runs in the family. Who knows?"

Mathilde turned to him, indomitable now, and gave him a vicious blast of rapid, furious French.

Then she turned back to Graham with as much colour in her face as he'd seen all day. "I'm sorry, *Inspecteur*," she offered. "My husband sometimes does not think before he speaks. George was a decent and loving man who would have made an excellent husband for Marie." Antoine sat in stony silence, the occasional twitch of his moustache being the only sign that he disagreed with her.

"Where were you both when George fell to his death?"

"In bed, of course. It had been a long day and late night," Antoine replied.

Mathilde nodded. "We were sleeping in. I was so very tired. I had been working for that day for weeks."

"Very well. I think that will do for now." As he stood to show the couple out, Graham thanked them both.

"*Ce n'est rien*," Mathilde assured him. "But I hope that you will also speak to George's sister. She was the one who understood George's... state of mind... from back then, when they were children, no?"

"What about Marie?" Antoine inquired. "What will happen to her? I don't like leaving her here. She is not herself."

"Don't worry. We'll take good care of her. You go back to the White House Inn and we'll be in touch," Graham said. He was keen to see the back of these complicated people. He could only imagine the fiery bickering that would probably dominate the rest of the couple's day. "Good day, now," he said as he ushered them from the station.

When he returned to his desk, he saw that two phone messages were awaiting him; one from Marcus Tomlinson, the other from Constable Roach. He called the pathologist first.

"Marcus? What's new over there? We're having the strangest of days, I can tell you, and I'd love some nice, straightforward, concrete evidence."

Tomlinson made an apologetic noise. "Sorry, old boy. I've done an advanced tox screen and a few other tests at my discretion. He wasn't drugged or poisoned. His hands hadn't been tied, and he wasn't gagged. No signs of struggle or a fight. All a bit of a puzzle really. It's as though he just toppled over for no reason at all."

Graham closed his eyes and considered a more colourful oath before uttering simply, "Bugger."

"I don't make it up, I just report it," Tomlinson said apologetically.

"It's alright. Just need a break, in every sense of the word," Graham confessed. "Say, whilst we're talking, do you know of a local headshrinker named...," Graham looked at the name on one of the bottles of pills that Marie Ross had been taking, "Bélanger?"

"Psychiatrist, you mean?" Tomlinson thought for two seconds. "Ah, yes. Has an office in St. Helier."

"You rate him?"

"I do. A good egg, by all accounts. Thorough. Completely bilingual. Why?"

"He's been prescribing Marie Ross the full works for a few months now." Graham read a list of six medications from his notebook.

"Right, well, you'll want to have a word. A patient would have to be damned near cuckoo to require all that lot."

"You think so?" Graham pressed.

"Well... Doctors overprescribe these days. Lots of reasons why. But he must have thought there was good justification. I'd recommend having a discreet word. Mind, he'll be bound by doctor-patient confidentiality, so it's rather up to him how much he chooses to divulge."

"Well, let's hope he's feeling generous today, eh? Thanks, Marcus."

Graham called Dr. Bélanger's emergency number and left a request for his immediate presence at the station. If anyone could shed some light on Marie's inexplicable behaviour, it was her psychiatrist.

Graham used the radio for the next call. "Five-one-nine, come in?"

"Roach here, sir," the constable replied promptly.

"You called, young man?"

"Still at the castle, sir. Still looking for the musicians. Nobody's seen hide nor hair of them since they arrived. We've been down in the jail cells and everything, but there's nothing. We'll keep trying, sir."

"Good lad. Let me know if anything happens."

"Righto, sir. And... sir? Don't you think it's a bit odd?"

"What's that, Constable?" Graham cast a glance up at the ceiling momentarily. He would have physically mud-wrestled someone for a decent cup of tea.

"We get this odd incident with Mr. Ross, sir, and then four people go missing within hours of each other? Doesn't that feel a bit... well, *weird*, sir?"

Graham took another set of deep breaths. "Son, this whole day has been bloody weird. And if you set off on some paranormal train of thinking and decide the castle's got a *ghost* or some other ludicrous..."

"Oh, no, sir," Roach insisted. "Nothing like that.

It's just a hell of a coincidence, that's all. And I thought we didn't believe in those."

Graham smiled. *He's learning. Ever so slowly, but still.* "Keep at it, Constable. Let me know the minute you find any sign of them, alright?"

CHAPTER FOURTEEN

A PIERCING, HARROWING scream shook the quiet reception area. A door flew open and Detective Inspector David Graham dashed to the interview room to see what on earth had happened.

"It's okay, boss...," Harding said as he burst through the door. "Marie's just having a tough time."

"Bloody hell," Graham muttered. Marie Ross sat curled up on the floor in the corner of the room, her hands over her ears. "What did you say to her?"

Harding was a little red-faced, though it hadn't been her fault. "I mean.... She'd been talking about George in the past tense, and answering questions about him as if he were dead..." Harding began.

"...But she hadn't truly accepted it. Not even after seeing his body lying on the floor this morning," Graham finished for her.

"Shock, sir," Harding said. "Reckon it's sinking in now."

"Look..." Graham raced to form a plan which might help their investigation whilst protecting Marie from the worst of her demons. "Her doctor is on his way. Can you stay with her? Get her some water, maybe? Just keep her calm until he gets here."

Harding approached Marie and knelt beside her. "Would you like a glass of water, sweetheart?"

The distraught woman said nothing. She was crying, hiding her face in her hands.

"How about a cup of tea?"

Marie lashed out, kicking at Harding like a cornered animal and bellowing in incomprehensible French.

"Steady..." Harding told Marie after exhibiting some nifty footwork to avoid Marie's blows. "It's okay... we're here to help you, love."

Marie snarled again and tried to slap Harding's offered hand away. The sergeant straightened. "She's not in the mood, sir."

Graham had watched these developments from the doorway. "I'll say," he said, impressed by Janice's calm, composed manner in the face of such provocation.

Less assured, he had a try at getting through to their witness. "Marie? Your doctor will be here in just a few minutes. Dr. Bélanger tells me that you've been getting much better lately," he fibbed, he had yet to speak to the psychiatrist. "And he's looking forward to..."

Marie yelled at him, inconsolable, desperate. She lunged forward, trying to bite his hand. "Right, that's it," Graham decided, stepping back as he would from a snarling dog. "Sergeant, I'm sorry to do this, but we're going to place her in a holding cell until her shrink gets here."

"Okay, sir."

"If you can do it without cuffing her, great. But if need be..."

"Understood, sir." It took cajoling and more force than Harding would have liked, but they got Marie downstairs and into a cell within five minutes. By the time she was in the small, bare room, perhaps realising what was happening, the fight had largely left her. She was a little more docile. Still, Graham reasoned between deep breaths, he could take no risks with the safety of his officers.

Harding ensured that Marie had nothing with which she might harm herself before leaving her alone. Once outside the cell, Janice pushed a plastic beaker of cold water toward the prisoner through the hatch in the door. "Drink this, love, and breathe deep, okay?"

Graham watched with professional pride. "Well handled, Sergeant."

"It breaks my heart," Harding told him as they climbed the stairs together, "after the day she's had."

"It's not what we'd prefer," Graham agreed, "but it won't be for long."

The detective inspector's prediction was accurate. After only ten minutes in the cell, Marie seemed calm enough to talk to her psychiatrist, Dr. Bélanger who'd just arrived. Graham and Harding escorted him downstairs, adding only a little detail to Graham's earlier phone message.

"She's becoming more aware of events, but only gradually," Graham told him. "The shock, I think, really knocked her sideways. We've tried our best, but neither Sergeant Harding nor I are experts at this kind of thing."

Bélanger was well over six feet tall, but he had a soothing, gentle manner. He straightened his navy blue tie and strode into the holding cells area. "On the left," Harding told him. "Second door."

Bélanger opened the hatch and spoke to Marie. "*Madame* Ross?"

She began crying again, but Bélanger motioned to the officers that he would be quite alright.

"I would climb mountains," Graham told Harding as they left Bélanger to it, "for a cup of tea. There just hasn't been a moment."

"I'll do the honours, sir."

"She is borderline in many ways," Bélanger told them half an hour later. "She is suffering from clinical depression as well as generalised anxiety. She's had a couple of psychotic episodes in the past that have required hospitalisation, but with medication, support, and limited stress, she's able to function. Her husband's death, though, seems to have tipped her over the edge."

Harding listened carefully. Their little constabulary had brought in psychiatrists for several reasons during her tenure, and she always found what they had to say fascinating. Bélanger appeared thorough, professional, and knowledgeable, even if he did spout a few too many buzzwords for her liking. "We didn't want to put her in a cell, Doctor," Harding said.

"I don't think it exacerbated her condition," Bélanger assured them, although he appeared irritated by their treatment of his patient, "but I'm surprised by the sudden violence. It's not something I associate with Marie."

"Losing a loved one can turn a person into someone they don't recognise...." Graham began, but then stopped. Harding and Bélanger waited, but Graham seemed lost in thought.

"I recommend that you release Ms. Ross from the cell immediately. I will ensure that she receives her medication and move her to a psychiatric unit in St. Helier," Bélanger said, much to Graham's relief. He didn't want to be responsible for Marie Ross a moment longer than was necessary. Her unpredictability and lack of logic made him anxious. The psychiatrist continued."She may be of more help to you when she is stable. I'll let you know if she reaches a state where she can be interviewed. However, she is pretty traumatised, it might well be some time."

"Understood. Sergeant Harding can arrange her release. I'll leave you to it. Please keep in touch Dr. Bélanger." The two men shook hands and Graham excused himself. He could hear his phone ringing in his office.

"Mrs. Taylor?" Graham was surprised when he answered the phone. "Is everything alright?" He listened to Mrs. Taylor's agitated report. "We'll be right over, Mrs. Taylor."

"Trouble at the inn?" Harding asked appearing as he hung up.

"Something of a 'commotion,' according to Mrs. Taylor," Graham said. "George Ross' sister has just awoken."

CHAPTER FIFTEEN

"AM I SEEING things?" Harry kept saying. "Shine it over there again."

"The battery's at twenty-five percent, Harry," Marina reminded him. "Make this your last one, okay?"

Their scramble over the mound of rubble and masonry had been difficult, but all four had made it and were now in the much larger chamber beyond.

Using their phones they discovered that the chamber, perhaps twelve feet by fifteen but less than eight feet in height, was badly damaged by whatever calamity had befallen the smaller tunnel behind them. One wall had crumbled, leaving a gap at its very top that was around two feet high.

"It doesn't make sense," Harry said, nodding at

Marina to turn off the phone once more. "It looks as though the room's been divided into smaller chambers for some reason. Those walls are just piles of bricks up to the ceiling. They're not connected to the ceiling itself."

"Maybe that's why they toppled during the 'earthquake?'" Emily speculated.

"I guess so," Harry agreed.

"Looks like an opportunity to me," Leo offered. "If we can climb the wall, we should be able to get into the next section. Doesn't it seem lighter in there to you than it does in here?"

The four stood shoulder-to-shoulder in the gloom, peering at the gap in the far wall. "Can't tell," Harry admitted.

"Maybe," Marina said.

"It might just be that the room's got different contents or that the walls are a different colour. Impossible to say," Emily said.

"I know! Let's build a 'staircase.' It'll allow us to get a handhold on the cleft at the top of the wall and we'll be able to pull ourselves over."

"I'm in," Leo said.

"Me, too," Marina agreed.

Only Emily was a holdout. "I don't know..."

"Come on, Em," Harry said. "We're in no man's land here. Stranded. 'Who dares wins, eh?'"

"Oh go on, then," Emily conceded.

Working almost entirely in the dark and by memory, they located larger blocks displaced by the "earthquake" and placed them at the foot of the wall. It was exhausting work, hard on their hands and backs especially, and they desperately needed sustenance. They were running short of water, Harry's small bottle their only source. Leo handed around a packet of toffees. It was only a small one and he doled them out carefully.

With Harry having forgotten his phone and Emily insisting that they keep at least one as backup in the event the batteries of the others gave out, they could only use two phones as sources of light at once. Working as quickly as they could in the relatively tight space, the four found themselves bumping into each other in the gloom, and more than once, dropping rocks on each other's feet. After one testy exchange, they worked in pairs, with one person resting, and the fourth holding up the phones so they could see. They rationed short blasts of light, far too bright in this almost complete darkness, to find their way.

The "staircase" took shape. The quartet found they could move rocks around the tunnel without causing further collapse so began piling the larger ones in a layer about three feet wide at the base of the wall they were attempting to climb. On top of these were slightly smaller rocks, and they found a few with flat edges, suitable for a good foothold.

At one point in the rotation of roles, Leo and Marina found themselves sitting next to each other. Marina held the phone and guided Harry to and fro as he strained to bring more rocks across the chamber whilst Emily found smaller fragments to pack between the larger ones to create a stable platform.

"Feels a bit like one of those adventure holidays, doesn't it?" Marina said.

Leo marvelled at the analogy in the circumstances but played along. "Or those deathly dull team-building things where you go out into the woods and solve problems together."

"Yeah. They always sounded awful," Marina commented. "I'd almost prefer to be stuck down here." She paused, her voice cracking a little. "Almost."

Leo put an arm around her. "It's going to be fine. You'll see."

"Sure," she said without real confidence.

"And it'll make a great story, right? Imagine telling your students about this?"

Emily couldn't help but overhear, and her earlier resolution to remain upbeat left her momentarily. "You mean, tell them how we got stuck under a castle—like a bunch of idiots because one of us," she said, "decided that curiosity *wouldn't* kill his particular cat?"

Harry had his hand on her forearm in seconds. "Take it easy. We all agreed to come in here. And you have to admit," he said, resuming his work, "that this is *one hell* of a freak accident. I mean these walls have stood for centuries and they choose *today* to crumble?"

"I'm honoured," Marina quipped. She stood. "My shoulder's a bit better. I don't mind doing some of that levelling work, Emily."

Relieved, Emily took a seat by Leo. "You okay?" he whispered.

"Yeah," Emily replied. "This dust is playing merry hell with my allergies, though. Can hardly see straight, not that there's much to see. Don't suppose you've got any antihistamines lurking in your trouser pocket?"

"Sadly not," Leo confessed. "Hey, Harry? Want to take a break?"

They switched out regularly and within half an hour, their hands sore and scratched, the quartet had built a three-foot-tall platform on which to stand.

"Right, then. Who's going first?" Marina wanted to know.

"I'll go," Leo said. "I'm tallest, anyway."

There were no objections. Leo took advantage

of all the light they had—three phones' worth—as he found footholds among the pile of rocks they'd assembled. As he reached the top, he stretched upward to see if he could get a grip on the ledge of the fissure. The bricks—thick, old-fashioned ones, each with a maker's mark—had come away from the wall in a pattern that left decent handholds, and Leo found the edge of a flat surface.

"The mortar must have been terrible," he observed, calling down to them. "The wall fell away in a nice, neat chunk." He experimentally pulled himself up, testing to see if the wall would hold his weight, then heaved himself hard up the face of it.

"Just take it easy," Emily said.

As Leo pushed off, the rough-hewn platform beneath him gave way. His momentum lost, he struggled to get both hands on the fissure. One slipped immediately and the other couldn't get sufficient purchase. "I'm ... shoot... I'm going..." he wailed as he toppled back away from the wall and into the darkness below.

CHAPTER SIXTEEN

"OKAY MRS. TAYLOR, what's the story?" Graham asked a little wearily.

The proprietor of the White House Inn was at her wit's end. "I can't *have* these disturbances, Inspector Graham. It's not *right*," she insisted, wringing her hands. "This is a *respected* hotel, and it's *Sunday*, for the love of all that is holy."

Graham made a conciliatory face. The White House Inn and its long-suffering owner had indeed been handed far more than their fair share of troubles in the past six weeks. Mrs. Taylor was all too aware that the impact of negative buzz on social media could mean ruin. Gorey was hardly experiencing a crime wave, but two mysterious deaths in as many months were two more than was reasonable for somewhere so idyllic.

"Why don't you just tell me what happened?" Graham said, notebook at the ready.

"She woke up." Marjorie Taylor sniffed. "Well after lunchtime."

"Who did?"

"Eleanor, Mr. Ross's sister," Mrs. Taylor said. "She knew nothing of the whole business regarding his death, she was just sleeping off a hangover. I suppose she has a phone. Anyway, she woke up and suddenly finds out about her poor brother."

"Quite the shock," Graham imagined. "What happened?"

"She was *screaming the place down!*" Mrs. Taylor informed him. "Completely lost her mind. Tearing around the hallways, yelling for her brother, for her parents, kept saying, 'Not again, not again.' I really didn't know what to make of it. We got her back into her room, and one of the staff is sitting with her now."

With a heavy sigh, Graham made a note of the room number and headed upstairs. Harding joined him after checking the guesthouse register.

"Once we've calmed Eleanor down," Harding told him as they climbed the stairs, "we've got Juliette, the victim's first wife, his new sister-in-law as it were, to deal with." She shook her head in wonderment.

"Oh," Graham said, simply. More complications. *Would this day ever end?*

Janice did the knocking. Eleanor's room was three doors down from the Jouberts' suite, but she had slept through alarms, nearby police visits, and the reports of tragedy on her phone. She had essentially received this avalanche of news and sympathy in the seconds after waking up with a ferocious hangover.

"Police?" Eleanor appeared to cling to the doorframe.

"May we come in, Ms. Ross?" Harding asked her gently. Graham was relieved to see that the emotional maelstrom described by Mrs. Taylor seemed to have passed for the moment.

Eleanor opened the door wide to let them in. Polly, the breakfast waitress had been sitting with Eleanor, and now slipped quietly past her. She looked greatly relieved. Polly acknowledged Graham with a slight nod as she passed into the hotel corridor.

"Polly," he responded. When she had gone, Harding and Graham went into the room and cast a better look at their victim's sister.

"I'm just... This is all just too much right now," Eleanor Ross said, on the edge of tears. She looked pretty awful, bleary-eyed, and fair hair askew, the very picture of a hung-over woman in her late twenties who didn't party very often and was suffering the consequences.

"This is a very difficult time, Ms. Ross. We don't want to make things any harder."

"Do you know what *happened*?" she said, slumping down onto the bed. She'd thrown on some jeans and a t-shirt, but she still looked thoroughly crumpled. Mascara smudged the soft skin under her eyes.

"He fell," Graham said, trying to find the gentlest of explanations, "at the castle. We aren't certain yet as to the circumstances."

"Fell?" she repeated. "George?"

"I'm afraid so."

Eleanor pursed her lips, holding back her emotions rather better than she had an hour earlier. "Did he... Did he jump?"

Harding handled this. "There's no evidence of that."

"An accident, then?" she tried next. "Maybe he slipped and..."

"We really can't say that, either," Harding told her.

Now Eleanor looked at them both, fixing them with eyes that were dulled of all sparkle. "Pushed?"

she brought herself to say. "Someone *pushed* George off the..."

"Again," Graham interrupted, his hands raised to stymie this train of thought before it could proceed, "we have no evidence. No one saw the incident occur. I was there but found him after he had fallen."

"You did?" Eleanor said, latching onto this fact. "Did he say anything?"

Graham shook his head. "I'm afraid not. His injuries were very serious."

"But he was alive?" It seemed particularly important that Eleanor understand these details, though Harding couldn't help finding her curiosity a little unusual. Even slightly morbid.

"He had no pulse," Graham related, "and he wasn't breathing. Like I say, he'd fallen from a considerable height and was badly injured. There was nothing anyone could have done," Graham assured her.

Eleanor sat on the edge of the bed, her shoulders slumped. She pinched the bridge of her nose, fighting both grief and a savage headache. "Poor boy," she said, more than once, closing her eyes. "Poor, poor boy. He overcame so much... Did so well for himself. He practically raised his daughter alone, you know, with Juliette off doing her own thing." Her feelings about her sister-in-law were obvious. "Then when she divorced him, he hardly got to see her. He was a hero too, you know. Saved some French kids from drowning."

Then the questions returned. It seemed that Eleanor simply had to understand this tragedy before she could begin to accept it. "What time did he fall?"

Graham checked his notebook, "It's difficult to say precisely, but I found him shortly after eight-thirty this morning."

Eleanor considered this. She looked at her watch. "I think I know what happened."

Harding and Graham exchanged a glance, both of them desperate for some movement in this fraught and awkward case. "Go on, Ms. Ross," Graham told her.

CHAPTER SEVENTEEN

STEPHEN JEFFRIES SAT in his office wracking his brains. Across the simple black desktop Constables Roach and Barnwell observed the fretting figure and, as they were trained to do, wrote down everything he said that was of value. The problem for them both was that, especially when nervous, Jeffries spoke in a ceaseless, excited torrent.

"I don't know how helpful I can be," he said, well into the fourth minute of a protracted, stream-of-consciousness monologue. "They played beautifully at the wedding, went back to their hostel afterward, and then apparently visited the castle this morning. I don't remember seeing them after I paid them for their stellar work," he said, glancing around the room like a distracted squirrel. "What I can provide, though, are photos of the quartet playing at the wedding reception." He promptly forwarded them to Roach from his phone.

The younger constable had done most of the talking—that which could be fitted in edgewise between Jeffries' nervous diatribes—and possessed a commitment to finding the missing foursome that suggested his career depended on it. Barnwell, in contrast, regarded the investigation as a waste of police time. "They're musicians, right?" he'd confirmed. "They'll be down the pub, getting hammered, spending whatever dosh they made last night at the wedding."

Roach, however, was a lot more concerned. Jeffries had left them in no doubt that, particularly for the curious with a disdain for closed doors and proscriptive signs, the castle could be an endless source of amusement. He had visions of the four musicians locking themselves into some ancient basement or falling down a poorly lit spiral staircase, nursing broken limbs and worse whilst vainly calling for help. The thought chilled him.

"Well," Roach reminded Barnwell with a persnickety wave of his pencil, "The lady on the front desk definitely saw them come in, but she did not see them leave."

"So she says, and I believe her," Jeffries agreed.

He looked harassed, his hair ever so slightly out of place. This was most uncharacteristic and indicated that today had been the rarest of days, one on which Stephen Jeffries found himself genuinely flustered by one event after another.

"We'll search the grounds again. Would you like to accompany us?" Roach offered. He didn't need to look over at Barnwell to understand the older man's utter contempt for what he saw as a senselessly wasteful plan.

"I wouldn't want to be in the way, but if I can be helpful," Jeffries replied, "I certainly will." Jeffries stood and put on a cardigan he usually only wore in the office. He led the two constables out of the office.

Jeffries took the two police officers around the quadrangle where the wedding had taken place. It was deserted now. Roach and Barnwell looked around. The grounds were immaculate. Not only was the castle a massive monument, but the staff recognised the importance of maintaining the dignity of this historic landmark. "Putting their best foot forward," as Jeffries referred to it.

"I'm glad to see that the remaining guests have resisted the temptation to simply mill about near the scene of the accident... or should that be *crime scene*.... No, no Stephen, let's not put the cart before the horse. *Scene of the accident* will do for now." Stephen Jeffries was mostly talking to himself. Like Mrs. Taylor, he was intensely anxious that a mysterious, sudden death should not unduly colour the public's opinion of this fine place.

"That's four times," Barnwell reminded Roach quietly when they had finished scouring the castle's exterior. "If you want to do a fifth tour of the grounds today, you'll do it alone."

"Right," Roach agreed, though he found Barnwell's habitual laziness particularly unhelpful today. "Let's head inside." He turned to Jeffries. "Where do the tourists normally go?"

Jeffries led them into the darker, cooler interior of the castle. The temperature dropped significantly, and all three men were glad of the respite from what had become an unseasonably warm day. "The old jail cells," Jeffries explained.

"Wonder if our missing quartet have managed to lock themselves in?" Barnwell offered.

Jeffries double-checked each cell, accompanied by Roach. "I'm afraid that's impossible. They can't be opened without one of the master keys." He led them down the narrow hallway, lit by wall-mounted electric lights that had taken the place of the flaming torches that had so long ago illuminated these ancient chambers.

"Is it worth calling their names?" Roach asked.

Jeffries felt it was worth a try. "Emily!" he

called down the hallway, listening to the dull, stony echo. "Marina!" he tried next. All three men listened carefully for a response, but none came. Jeffries shrugged and led them onward.

They passed a closed-off room that Jeffries explained was earmarked as the home of their new torture exhibit. "Fantastic," Barnwell said. "Maybe they're torturing each other for fun."

The door to it was closed, but Jeffries stopped. "The sign barring people from entering has been moved." Ever a stickler for details, he slid it back into place. "Probably some kids. The room's not open yet. And what with today's accident, I'm not sure it ever will be."

"Pity," Barnwell said. "A little S&M never hurt anyone, right? Let's have a little look-see."

Roach rolled his eyes but opened the door to the exhibit. The three men went inside. The room was completely dark and smelled musty. Dust tickled their noses. "This is going to set me off," Roach complained, shielding the lower part of his face with his hand.

"Emily!" Jeffries yelled again.

"If it turns out," Constable Barnwell told his colleague, "that they're *actually* down the pub, you owe me dinner at the Bangkok Palace."

Forgetting the dust in his irritation, Roach put

his hands on his hips. "Can we *please* focus on the..."

"With drinks," Barnwell underlined. "Lots of them."

"I thought you were off the sauce?" Roach whispered back as Jeffries poked around the darkened room.

"Ow!" they heard him say.

Both officers were alert. "You alright, sir?" Roach asked, shining his torch in Jeffries' direction.

"Yes, yes," Jeffries said, a little embarrassed. "Just caught myself on this pike." Roach illuminated the 17th century weapon, a five-foot-long wooden shaft topped with a truly nasty-looking sharpened spike. "Oof. Wouldn't want to get on the wrong end of one of *those*."

"Shall we?" Barnwell, suddenly tired of investigating the exhibit, urged the others toward the door and back into the relative comfort of the hallway.

Jeffries wrung his hands. "Where on *earth* have they got to?"

CHAPTER EIGHTEEN

ELEANOR ROSS SAT up straight and took a deep breath. "You know that this was George's second marriage, right?"

"Yes," Harding acknowledged. "He was married to Marie's sister."

"And how do you think," Eleanor said testily, "that his druggy, ne'er-do-well ex-wife felt about *that*?"

Graham raised one eyebrow. "Well, you know her better than we do, Ms. Ross."

"She overreacts to things," Eleanor explained. "She can be as cool as a cucumber for ages, then she suddenly goes off the deep end for no reason. I mean, neither of the Joubert daughters are particularly stable, but Juliette was always someone about whom you wonder... you know, not *if* something bad is going to happen, but *when*. Constantly treading on eggshells George was, both before and after their divorce."

Harding handled the next question. "And you believe she might have had something to do with George's death?"

The word, *death*, incontrovertible and so shockingly *final*, stabbed at Eleanor. She took a moment to collect her emotions once more. Harding reproached herself. Perhaps next time she'd choose a euphemism. *Demise* might have been better, she reasoned. Or even just *an accident*.

"She certainly didn't like the idea of George marrying Marie. Even though it was her who left him. I'm not certain, of course, but if I were investigating, I'd want to have a serious word with her." Aggression seeped into Eleanor's tone.

"Ms. Ross," Graham said sternly, "I urge you not to make a bad situation worse."

"No, no," Eleanor said as she stood. "I understand. I'm not a violent person, mister, erm..."

"Detective Inspector Graham," he reminded her.

"Right. Juliette has nothing to fear from me. Perhaps from the law, but not from me."

Harding noticed that Eleanor's fists were balled tightly. She found herself not caring much for this young woman only slightly younger than herself. She tried to regard the distressed woman kindly, but there was now an air of revenge about her as if she had decided for herself what kind of disaster had befallen her brother and who had caused it.

"If you'd rather," Graham said, his tone even, "take a break, gather your thoughts, get something to eat. We can talk shortly."

"No, no, you need my help," Eleanor insisted, "I know the people involved. Juliette, her meddling parents. Even that Marie. *None* of them are in their right minds, you know."

Graham could see Eleanor quickly cycling through the emotions of grief, jealousy, and anger. All were interspaced with moments of calm and lucidity, a common reaction to unbearable news. "Is that so?"

"Juliette's nasty, spiteful. And Marie's *crazy!*" Eleanor said, suddenly rising and stomping around the room. "*Certifiable,*" she underlined. "She's depressed one day and on cloud *nine* the next. She treated George like a leper, then like a saint, then like someone she couldn't *stand,* then," she said, spittle flying as she raged, "like someone she couldn't live without!"

"Please, Ms. Ross," Graham tried.

"You've got to listen. They all drove him to it. Or they did it themselves. That family is *poisonous.*" Barely pausing for breath, Eleanor now seemed content to let her every thought tumble out, as though her brother's death had burst a dam and unleashed a torrent. Which, of course, it had....

"And the Jouberts?" Harding prompted. She was learning that with cooperative witnesses like Eleanor, it was often sufficient to toss them the occasional encouraging prompt to elicit information. She thought of it as adding a squirt of lubricant so that the mechanisms would keep turning smoothly. So it was with Eleanor.

"*He's* a prig with a chip on his shoulder, despite his affectations," she told them. "And *she's* this weird, controlling, mother-hen figure," she added flapping her hands.

Graham was noting this down with speed and precision. "But they never displayed any open hostility toward George?"

Another angry shrug. "Only on a daily basis," Eleanor grumbled. "You know how some parents are. 'Zer's not a man in ze world who's good enough for my leetle gurrl.' All of that nonsense. Him, especially. As though his daughters were the finest catches in all of France."

"And it's not just this, the two weddings, the weird relationships with the sisters. It's the old stuff. With our parents. Back in France." Now Eleanor paused for a second, but neither police officer acknowledged her point. "You *must* have heard about that," she whined. "Didn't anyone tell you?"

Caught between two competing needs, Graham tried to keep Eleanor calm. At the same time, he was desperate for the effusive, unwittingly helpful Eleanor to simply *keep talking*.

"The accident at the farmhouse, you mean?" Graham said, motioning for Eleanor to sit back down on the bed. He'd have given anything to beam them all to the station, but this wasn't the time.

Eleanor ignored his gesture and paced the room. "That's one word for it," she said. "It's always been incredibly hard for me to believe that my father would have done something like that."

Eleanor finally sat down, palm to her forehead. Neither Harding nor Graham saw any theatre in it. The woman was clearly suffering, and the pounding champagne headache could not have been helping her state of mind.

"I'll fetch you some water," Harding offered. She fished a painkiller from a stash in her bag and brought a glass of water from the bathroom. Eleanor's emotional state seemed, in the face of this kindness, to drop a couple of gears. Her shoulders sagged. "Thanks," she said her tone low. "Please, I need time to process this. I am exhausted."

"We'll speak with Juliette and check in with

you later," Graham said gently. "If there's anything you need, I'm sure Mrs. Taylor will help."

The two officers made to leave, but Graham felt a hand on his arm. Eleanor looked up at him with luminous eyes. "Look... I'm sorry. It's all too much."

"I do understand," Graham said with sincerity. "Believe me."

"Whatever happened, I know that George didn't kill himself," Eleanor said, her eyes beginning to moisten. "He wouldn't. Not him. He knew what it would do to... you know... the people left behind. After... before."

Graham nodded. "We'll do everything we can." Eleanor returned to staring at the floor, holding her aching temples, whilst Graham and Harding took their leave, closing the door quietly behind them.

CHAPTER NINETEEN

T HE TWO OFFICERS collected themselves. Graham readied a new page in his notebook, but they resisted the temptation to indulge in a discussion in such a public place.

"And now," Graham said with a funny smile, "for something completely different."

Harding remained deadpan.

"*Monty Python?*" Graham asked, incredulous. "Please don't tell me seventies comedy completely passed you by?"

"Not my thing, sir," Harding replied.

Graham tutted quietly. "My dear sergeant. You simply haven't lived." He wrote a few words in his notebook.

"Now for Juliette."

"Juliette, sir."

Graham raised his hand to knock, but his phone buzzed. "Hang on. This might be Tomlinson again."

It wasn't. It was Graham's contact with the French police. Their conversation was a little longer this time, and Graham squinted as he listened. "Thank you, *Monsieur*," he said. "Most interesting."

Graham took Harding by the elbow and walked a few doors down the hallway. He spoke quietly to her. "Remember the business with George's parents over in France?"

Harding nodded. "Did Poirot have something else for us?"

"No kidding," Graham replied. "Guess—I'm serious, just guess—who do you think owned the farm *right next door* to the one where the Ross parents were found dead?"

Harding blinked. "No way."

"Way," Graham assured her.

"The *Jouberts*?" she asked. "How about that?"

"How, indeed," Graham replied. "That must be how George and the two sisters first met."

Harding brought out her tablet and with the information Graham gave her, she produced a map of the area. "Right next door. You'd actually have to walk or drive through the Joubert's property," Harding noted, tracing the map with her fingertip, "to get to the main road. The two families must have been very close."

"Especially as the Ross clan were there almost every summer, so Poirot said."

Harding chewed this over. "What did he say about the evidence?"

"That's where things get murky," Graham replied. "Ross senior's fingerprints were on the gun. Once the murder-suicide theory became the dominant idea, they didn't look for any other explanation. Interviewed everyone in the area, apparently, then called it what they called it and closed the book."

"But your Poirot doesn't buy the theory?" Harding speculated.

"He's on the fence. Said it just didn't smell right. Bereaved families say this kind of thing as a matter of course, but it seems the Ross parents truly *were* a happy couple, adored George and his little sister Eleanor, loved the French countryside, were financially stable, all the rest of it."

"There was one more thing," Graham added. "The esteemed *Monsieur* Joubert has a chequered past."

"Oh?"

"He was involved in some kind of incident with a former business associate."

"Interesting."

"He was implicated but never charged in the stabbing of said business associate."

"Wow." Harding made a note. "Sounds like Antoine has a temper. Hope it doesn't run in families, or this is going to be another bloody awkward interview."

Graham nodded, pulled himself up tall as he often did when approaching a potentially awkward situation, and knocked on the door. Harding was reminded of those animals that try to make themselves look large and fierce in the face of a predator.

In this case, their foe was Juliette Paquet, formerly Ross, née Joubert. She appeared at the door, an almost mirror image of her sister—the same long, dark, straight hair, the blue eyes. "Who are you?" she asked, none too politely, her accent very thick.

"Gorey Police, ma'am," Graham said, producing his ID. "We'd like to speak with you about the death of..."

"I was going for coffee," she said. She made to push past them.

"Please wait," Graham said. "This won't take long."

"I need coffee," she repeated. She didn't meet their eyes. It was, Harding felt, like arguing with a truculent teenager, one who simply couldn't *believe* they were grounded again.

"May I suggest room service?" Harding tried.

Now Juliette stared at Harding as though meeting a new adversary for the first time. She turned on her heel and waved them in with little more than a grunt, taking a seat by the window. The curtains were closed and her posture sagged, her shoulders hunched. The room had the visibility of a house where the kitchen was on fire, the smoke acrid and pungent. Graham saw that Juliette had been working steadily through a pack of high-tar French cigarettes.

"I wonder," Graham began, "if we might open a window?

Juliette gave them another noncommittal shrug, a gesture that struck Harding as unmistakably French. Graham popped open all the windows, though he stopped short of drawing back the curtains completely. A great welter of sunlight would have been entirely incompatible with Juliette's jet-black mood and probably her entire existence.

Juliette's room was markedly smaller than both Graham's and the more comfortable suite Juliette's parents occupied. She sat in the only chair. The two officers stood, not comfortable with sitting on the bed. They found themselves being unselfconsciously ignored by Juliette, who lit up another cigarette and puffed on it disdainfully.

"We'd like to extend our condolences," Harding began. "This must be a very difficult day."

"What do you want to know?" Juliette interrupted rudely. "What do you think I can tell you?" She puffed out smoke, the acrid fumes curling around her nose and ears.

Graham adopted a sterner tone. "What time did you leave the wedding party last night?"

That shrug again. Graham analysed it, absorbing the details.

"Late," she said. "Maybe three. There was music and champagne. Why would anyone want to leave?"

"And where were you," Graham asked next, "at around eight-thirty this morning?"

Juliette blew out another great cloud of grey-purple smoke and slightly inclined her head toward the room's unmade bed. "I was asleep."

Graham made a note. "How did you hear about the tragedy at the castle?"

This brought Juliette to a halt. She stubbed out the rest of her cigarette and turned to Graham. "Tragedy?" she asked, raising an eyebrow.

"Yes, the death of..."

"I know who died. And I know when. My mother told me."

"How?" Harding wanted to know.

There were more truculent teenage gestures—rolled eyes and a pout. "She knocked on the door," Juliette said as if explaining the situation to a child. "She said, 'Juliette, George has fallen off the castle. He is dead.' Then I went back to sleep."

Both officers were reading this young woman, her behaviour, her accent, and her lack of interest in helping them. Both were privately elevating her up their list of suspects.

"Do you believe it possible that George committed suicide?" Harding asked.

Another shrug. "People get sad. Maybe life with Marie wasn't so perfect."

Graham got straight to the point. "Were you jealous of your sister?" Juliette's eyes darted around to focus on him. "After all, he had been your husband once."

There was a brief explosion of French. Harding recognised a couple of curses. Then Juliette said, "He was a *nobody*! Not even a real man."

Harding felt a new and genuine sympathy for poor George who seemed, despite his being in the centre of it, largely forgotten, dismissed, or otherwise defamed in this family of big, complicated egos. She'd never imagined that the victim of a sudden and mysterious incident like this one should find himself so badly maligned by those who might be expected to mourn him. First Antoine and now Juliette, not to mention Marie. For a family into which he'd married not once but *twice*, several of them appeared to have the lowest opinion of George Ross.

"But yet you attended their wedding. Travelled here, booked a hotel, took a full part in the celebrations," Graham reminded her. "You left the daughter you shared with Mr. Ross in France.

Juliette was surrounded by thick smoke, as though she were a conjurer whose trick had gone wrong, but she made no attempt to wave it away, apparently inured to the poisonous atmosphere. "I knew there would be free champagne."

"And the reason for leaving your daughter behind?"

"The wedding of her father to her aunt wasn't the place for my daughter. She is sensitive. These things are complicated. Adult things, you know?"

"But your sister..." Harding began.

"Is an idiot," Juliette spat. "I told her what she was getting into, and she didn't listen. She *never* listens. We haven't had a proper conversation in years."

"What *was* she getting into, Ms. Paquet?" Graham used the silence that followed to take stock. In the end, he boiled his thoughts down to a single

question: "Juliette, can I ask what you think happened to George?"

One more shrug. Did it mean *I don't know* or *I
don't care?* Graham felt it might be a mixture of the
two. Juliette had shown no grief over her ex-husband's loss, no sympathy for her sister, only contempt for the emotions that always swirled around a
sudden death. It was as if she'd been here a hundred
times and was simply bored of it all.

"Maybe he was drunk and leaning over the
side," Juliette pondered. "Or maybe he slipped. I
have no idea. You're the detectives," she said,
lighting up another cigarette. "You figure it out."

Ten minutes later, Graham paced around the patio
terrace of the White House Inn waiting for Constable
Roach to pick up his blessed phone. He gratefully
filled his lungs with fresh afternoon air. It had been a
long time since he'd been in so smoky an environment
as Juliette's room, and he knew the smell would linger
on his clothes and his skin until he could shower.

"Constable Roach, I'm going to listen for a brief
moment whilst you tell me that your missing persons case is concluded."

"Ah," Roach began. "Erm."

"Oh, for the love of God, Roach," Graham muttered. "We need to interview twenty more wedding guests. I'm up to my ears in Gallic disinterest and sociopathic siblings. I need some good news. Lay it on me."

Roach explained the situation, none too proud of their having come up short, but unable to improve on the reality. "We've turned the place upside down, sir. No one's seen them, and they're not in any of the basement hallways."

Uncharacteristically, but in a moment that spoke of the stress and confusion of the day, Graham unleashed a brief, colourful torrent of vernacular.

"You alright, sir?" Roach asked.

Graham took six long breaths, so deep and determined that Roach heard every one. "Constable Roach, I need several things in short order. I need a pot of tea so badly that I'd threaten Mrs. Taylor with a loaded gun if she told me that the kitchen had run out of Oolong. I need the witnesses in this case to do a bit more *witnessing* and the family to be a damned sight more *familial*." Roach knew venting when he heard it, and he stood quietly, phone to ear, letting his boss get things off his chest. "I need the esteemed Marcus Tomlinson to get back to me with something more concrete than, 'Sorry, DI Graham, this bloke's dead, and I don't know why.'

And," he pushed on, "I need my crack team of missing persons experts to find some *bloody missing people!*"

"Roger that, sir," Roach could only say.

"Get on with it," Graham told him. "I hope there remains not an iota of confusion as to what I need from you, son."

"Absolutely none at all, sir."

Click.

CHAPTER TWENTY

IN THE DARKNESS, Marina cradled Leo in her lap and made him as comfortable as she could. Harry's sweater, donned that morning in case the castle inner hallways were chilly, made a serviceable blanket but they were very short of other ways to keep him warm.

"I'm telling you," Marina kept saying, "I heard something."

Harry alternated between kneeling, concerned about the stricken Leo, and trying to bolster the improvised staircase from which his friend had fallen. "All I heard," Harry said honestly, "was Leo yelling because he'd just broken his arm."

Emily, never one to let sloppy summations slip

by, replied. "You're not a doctor. We don't know what's happened to his arm."

Harry was miffed. "Look at the angle of it." He shined a light on Leo's forearm. It was slightly bent and rapidly swelling above the wrist. "Does that look like an unbroken arm to you?" The stress of their predicament was getting to them all. Tempers were beginning to fray.

"Okay, okay, let's keep calm," Leo's pained voice rose from the dusty floor of the chamber. It was almost the first thing he'd managed to say since falling, twenty minutes earlier, except to repeatedly apologise for making their already bad situation markedly worse.

Despite the bickering, Marina was adamant about her earlier claim. "It sounded like someone shouting from back there," she said, nodding toward the pile of rocks that was all that remained of the tunnel through which they'd arrived.

Emily shrugged, unwilling to rule anything out. "Point is, we didn't reply."

"We were a little distracted," Harry said defensively, motioning to Leo's arm. It was lying across his chest in what had become the least painful position. "I thought he was out cold," he added. In the moments after Leo's fall and before light could be brought to where he had landed, it had indeed seemed that Leo was knocked unconscious. They had scrambled over to help him but found he was simply stunned. He had taken a long moment to realise what had happened, and before he was truly aware, Marina, a former Queen's Guide, was soon attending to his arm.

"Well, even if they are looking for us down here, I say we continue to try getting over into the next chamber," Harry said.

But Emily remained unconvinced. "There's no guarantee that the next chamber is any improvement on this one. Or that we could get Leo over the wall."

"We wouldn't have to," Marina told her, "if Harry could find a way out and get help." It was hard to counter the logic of her statement.

There seemed no reason to debate any further. Emily, still full of misgivings, inspected Harry's replacement "staircase," which was only a slightly more secure version of the rock pile Leo had climbed. "One foothold after another," she advised. "Super slow and careful. And I want you to agree to abort this mission if you find there is no safe way down into the chamber on the other side."

"Yes, Mother," Harry quipped as he began his ascent. The augmented rocks would take him just a little higher than the point Leo had reached, but should, he hoped, make the job of levering himself into the next chamber quite a lot easier. What would happen from there onward, of course, no one could say.

The three left behind waited as Harry steadily made his way up the pile of rocks, using specially built footholds. They were making progress much easier. One of their three phones was now below twenty percent power, so Emily turned it off and used hers to light Harry's way. He had the other phone, and she hoped it would reveal some good news when he got to the gap at the top of the wall and could see into the next chamber.

"Okay, I've got a good grip," he said, reaching the jagged gap where the wall of the chamber had crumbled. "Here goes."

Harry hauled himself up so that the top of the wall, two bricks thick and noticeably shoddily made, was under his belly. He paused there. "Hey... You know what?"

"You okay?" Emily called up.

"There's a big pile," Harry called back, his voice constrained by his curious embrace of the wall, "of *boxes* in here."

Marina and Emily exchanged a glance. Leo had his eyes closed but was listening. "What kind?" Emily cried.

"Wooden," came the reply. "Big, solid things."

"Is there a way out? How does the rest of the room look?" Marina was desperate to know.

"Like..." Harry began, and then pulled himself further over so that he could reach down and brace himself against one of the boxes. "You remember... the end of that movie?" His voice was muffled.

"Which movie?"

"*Indiana Jones*," Harry replied, levering himself fully over the wall and standing straight up on the closest wooden box. The pile must have been ten feet high, perhaps more. "You know, the huge room full of wooden boxes where they store the Ark of the Covenant? Bloody good movie." He was shouting now.

Emily and Marina exchanged another glance. "Sure," Emily humoured him.

"That's what it looks like in here," Harry said, shining his phone light around the chamber. "Dozens of them. In stacks, against the walls." He looked around, then down. "I think I can get down to the floor." He was panting and sweaty with effort.

"Okay," Emily shouted. Their voices were noticeably harder to discern through the wall of the chamber, and she found herself nearly screaming at him. "Just go slowly and watch your footing."

Harry didn't reply but was grateful to find the way down easily. Within moments, he'd stepped from the pile of boxes and was in the middle of the room. Above him, he noticed, was a single light bulb suspended from the ceiling. "There might even be light in here. Hang on."

Miraculously, in perhaps the best news they'd had since the rockfall hours earlier, the light still worked. "Eureka!" he cried. "I haven't seen a door yet, but this place is pretty interesting. Wonder what's in these boxes?"

"Markings," Leo said quietly.

"Any markings on them?" Marina called, grateful now for her voice coaching lessons. She'd taken them originally to help her with speaking to audiences during concerts, but now found they were excellent for learning to project in underground chambers. Who knew?

Harry put away the phone and took a close look at the nearest boxes. "This one says 'E.E.R.,'" he said. "The font looks a bit familiar. I think I've seen that in a movie, too. Oh, wait…" There was a pause.

"Harry?" Marina yelled. The only response was a creaking sound, something like wood being broken. "Harry, I'm serious, if you release mustard gas or start a nuclear chain reaction in there, we'll have *words* later."

The voice that came back was not at all jocular. "I think you need to come over here."

"Seriously?" Emily said.

"Yes," Harry confirmed. "All of you."

"But Leo..." Marina objected.

"Him too," Harry told them. "Find a way, and do it right now."

CHAPTER TWENTY-ONE

EVENTS BOTH LARGE and small had done much to undermine Detective Inspector David Graham's enduring belief in a benevolent God, but a well-timed and perfectly-brewed pot of tea did much to reaffirm it. How, he speculated as he poured his third cup with a steady hand, could such an extraordinary and healthful tonic be available to humanity except through the guidance of a loving Creator?

Janice spotted his mood. "Thinking big thoughts?" she asked as she sat down. After a hectic day, they were back at the station and she'd taken the time to put on her spare uniform. She was now at her resplendent best, her hair neatly tied back and eyes sparkling.

"Just putting some more fuel in the tank," Graham told her. "I suspect our day's work is far from finished."

"I learnt recently that the chances of an interviewee either forgetting something or embellishing the truth increase exponentially starting around twelve hours after the events in question," Janice said.

Graham nodded. "No eyewitness testimony can ever be regarded as one hundred percent accurate," he told her, "because we're relying on frail and fragile human beings."

"Makes you wish there were cameras everywhere," Harding offered. "It would cut crime in half."

Sipping his tea, Graham briefly thought this over, but having worked in London for so long, this topic was a well-trodden path. "At what cost?"

Harding replied, "They're not all that expensive, are they? And the information could cut down on investigative work and interviews, save us a ton of money..."

Graham raised a hand to bring her to a halt. "Police work is not," he said very seriously, "and never will be some kind of video game where you click a few buttons and suddenly you've got your suspect."

"Well, no, but..."

"And the idea that we might all have our every waking moment scrutinised by some looming, centralised authority is the pivotal script for every dystopian sci-fi novel ever written. That's how police states operate, Sergeant."

Chewing this over, Harding was forced to agree. "Yes, sir. The thing is, in cases like this, wouldn't it be helpful if there were a drone hovering over Gorey taking it all in? Or a bunch of cameras on the Orgueil battlements, filming everything that happens?"

"You know," Graham said, sitting back and pinching his nose, "when I first joined the force, we had to jump through a dozen fiery hoops to get a wiretap. It was almost unheard of. And not only was the technology rather flimsy and the legal side full of problems but there was an *ethical* side, too."

Harding listened, doing her best to imagine an earlier, more innocent time, probably just a few years before. After all, the DI wasn't that much older than she, no more than mid-thirties anyway. He just seemed older. He'd probably joined the force no more than fifteen years prior.

"After all, we were intercepting someone's personal correspondence. In doing so, we were breaching their privacy, and all because we *suspected* they were up to something. Convincing the judge each time was an absolute minefield."

"Really? It's a cinch these days, isn't it?" Harding remarked.

"Well, I can tell you, it took *ages* back then, and it wasn't that long ago. You had to stand there and swear up and down that the target was legitimate, that they'd definitely been involved in something or in touch with someone and then," he added, his fingers circling to evoke the endless nature of the process, "you had to sign documents detailing how you'd *treat* the information, who you could discuss it with, what you planned to do with it, the whole nine yards."

"Sounds like a giant pain in the bum," Harding said.

"Yes," Graham admitted. "But it was *police work*. It was genuine and thought through, and we only spied on people when we absolutely had to."

Harding wasn't prepared to let this one go. "So, you want to return to a time when we fill in a stack of paperwork just to listen to one individual's phone conversations?"

Graham knew there was no easy answer. "I'd like the process to be more efficient, but the same standards have to apply. Not some broad-ranging, bulk collection system that just sucks up everything pretty much indiscriminately."

"But if it did," Harding persisted, "we'd know

about crimes before they happened. We could prevent them."

"Maybe," Graham admitted cautiously. "But imagine this. Two friends are talking on the phone. They get into a discussion about how it might be nice to have a bit more money. One of them mentions that the corner shop has poor security, and the other one makes a snarky comment that the owner has been overcharging for years."

"Okay," Harding said, following intently.

"If the conversation stops at that point, and they *don't* rob the place, have they committed a crime simply by talking about it?"

"Not as the law currently stands," Harding had to admit.

"But we've made it our business to *listen* to them anyway," Graham said, tapping the table with a rigid index finger. "We acted as though they *were* committing a crime, *just in case they did.*"

Harding wasn't quite with him. "But if they *did* rob the shop, we'd have evidence pointing to them, and we'd be able to arrest them."

"For *having a conversation?*" Graham asked, incredulous. "Imagine that the shop had no CCTV and that no one there was able to identify the burglars. We'd have no evidence to make an arrest, just an illegally gathered phone conversation."

"Yeah, but at least we'd have it," Harding countered.

"So," the DI wanted to clarify, "in your perfect universe, overhearing two people talking about committing a crime would be sufficient to arrest them for having committed that crime?"

Harding was loathe to risk the disapproval of her boss, and she was on uncertain ground. "I don't know, sir. But it certainly would be more efficient."

"More efficient than what?"

"All the interviews and forensics and what-have-you," she replied.

Graham found that they had reached his main point, and he made it with the certainty of many years' thought and experience. "All of that *what-have-you* is the very definition of police work, Sergeant. We find out what *actually* happened, not what was *planned* to happen.

"We interview witnesses like the Jouberts and the people who work at the castle, to build up a picture of the suspects. We investigate the crime scene to see what it can tell us. We investigate facts, such as George having his own place and that Marie stayed elsewhere before the wedding. All of that takes time and effort, and it's a royal pain in the arse, I don't mind admitting," he said. "But it's *authentic*, and it doesn't invade anyone's privacy."

"But what if you don't get a conviction because

you're not permitted to gather stuff like phone data?" Harding said.

"Then we don't," Graham said. "Simple as that. We're going to catch whoever murdered George, if that's truly what happened, using the same methods of deduction and the same examination of evidence that have served investigators since the beginning. But if the conviction can't be had through fair means, it doesn't mean we should indulge in foul ones."

It was Harding's turn to be incredulous. "But then, the murderer might get away with it!"

Graham took a breath and chose to smile rather than continue down the road to anger, a journey he'd allowed himself to take far too often, despite never enjoying where it led. "People have been getting away with crimes since our ancestors established the principles of right and wrong. No justice system can catch every crook, nor should they try to. A good part of what we do, for better or worse, is *deterrence*."

Harding was nodding now. "Simply by being outstanding, professional investigators, we show the would-be criminals of the world that should they one day choose to be idiotic enough to commit a crime, we'll be all over them and won't rest until we've found what we need to get a conviction. In the process, we show that we act using only fair and authentic detection methods."

Harding reflected on this. Whenever she sat down with DI Graham, particularly when he was just finishing a big pot of tea, she always found that she learnt something, often something very significant that could change her worldview or explode a long-held myth. It was like having... she searched for the word... a *guru*.

"Hmm, I wonder, though," she cautioned, "if, in this particular case, someone thought they *could* get away with it. That we'd never find out."

The reminder of their current investigation was unwelcome, but timely. "Indeed, Sergeant Harding, indeed. I wonder. Let's go and find out, shall we?" They stood together.

"You know," Graham said. "I think I fancy another chat with the Joubert family. A longer chat. A one-to-one conversation with each of them, perhaps."

"Good idea, boss," Harding agreed.

"Because, and I've noted this before, as you'll recall, something *bloody funny* is going on with this case."

"Agreed, sir," Harding said, following him.

"And people don't just jump to their deaths for no reason. And they don't slip and fall from a walkway that has a two-foot thick medieval battle-ment all along its edge."

"They certainly don't, sir."

"And they assuredly don't get pushed off to their deaths, without someone *else* having a very good reason. In their minds, at least. Unless the castle had ghosts. And I don't believe in ghosts. Do you, Sergeant Harding?"

Janice found herself on an emotional pendu-lum, swinging between a renewed enthusiasm for cracking this case, and growing respect—yes, an ad-miration—for the remarkable mind of this man, her boss. When he was in this kind of form, he was simply unstoppable, and it was exhilarating to watch.

"Ghosts? No, sir. I don't, sir."

"Good. Let's get back to the White House Inn. I'll kick it off this time if you don't mind, Sergeant. I'm in a mood to be the one doing the talking."

CHAPTER TWENTY-TWO

T O THE RELIEF of the whole quartet, the journey into the next chamber was not nearly as awkward and painful as Leo had feared. The stability of the "staircase" was key. Conquering his apprehension of once more ascending the pile of rubble, Leo found a way to shuffle through the gap at the top of the wall where Marina and Harry received him and made sure he suffered no further injury.

"Top man," Harry said. "Sorry to make you go through all that, but I believe you'll thank me in a moment."

The room was perhaps twenty feet wide and twenty-five feet long, larger than where they had come from, and well lit, for a change. Stacked against all four walls were large wooden crates, each marked with the same three letters, "E.E.R."

"Are they connected to Queen Elizabeth? Marina asked.

"Hardly. That font is as German as they come," Leo replied. "Exactly the stereotypical Teutonic script."

"Jesus, Harry," Emily said, making her way down from the final box and arriving on the floor with a short jump. "This could be a haul of secret weapons or poison or something..."

"No," Harry said. "It most certainly isn't poisonous. Or dangerous." He paused, enjoying the moment. "Unless, of course, it's the late 1930s, and you're concerned about its potential influence on German culture."

"Eh?" Emily responded, but then turned to see the opened crate. Harry had unearthed its contents, removed the curtain-like packing material, and displayed three unframed paintings by propping them up against the case in which they'd remained hidden for at least seventy years.

Marina said it. "What," she began slowly, "the heck..."

"Franz Lipp," Leo told them proudly. "Austrian, born around 1890, if memory serves." With his good arm, he ushered the others out of his light and took a closer look. "Oh, yes," Leo grinned. "It's him, for certain. Look at these brush strokes. The confidence of an artist in his prime. And the colours," he pointed out, "vibrant, but serene."

Undimmed by the years, the painting was a composite of arching, looping swathes, purple and green, invoking a pastoral scene perhaps, with the whirl of a passing storm in the background. "He was Jewish, but before Hitler made his little power grab in 1933, Lipp's works found their way into some of Europe's finest collections. Including," he added meaningfully, "that of the Rosenberg family."

There was silence as the others struggled to understand. "Leo," Emily said, transfixed by the painting. "What exactly is going on here?"

Leo continued, full of energy now. "These other two are probably his as well. Although this one," he said, pointing to the smallest canvas, "might be by a student. Or it could be Lipp's earlier work. See how it's a little more pedantic, more obvious; *here*'s a harbour, and *here*'s a boat... Whilst in his later works, his style became so much more fluid and amorphous."

"'Degenerate art,'" Marina breathed. "The kind of paintings that were unacceptable in the Third Reich. The modernists, Cubists, Surrealists... Can you imagine that Picasso was *illegal?*"

Emily was flabbergasted. "You've got to be kidding me." She looked around the spartan chamber. "*Here?* Of *all places?*"

Harry shrugged. "Why not? The Germans knew that air raids or naval bombardment would only endanger the beleaguered Jersey public. The British wouldn't bother invading so they were as safe as houses here."

Her mind working at full speed, Marina said, "Wait, we never defended the island against the Germans? We just left the people here under *Nazi occupation?*"

Harry had read about the islands before leaving London and had a ready answer. "Couldn't be done. The Germans were well dug in, and it would have been a horrendous job to boot them out. Besides," he added, "the strategic importance of the islands was limited. The Germans occupied Jersey virtually unimpeded. So, this was as safe a place as any to store forbidden artworks."

"But why?" Emily said.

"Perhaps," Leo continued, "to sell after the war, or trade for more desirable works, as they so often did."

"Desirable?" Emily asked, taking a closer look at the paintings. "These are amazing."

"To us, sure," Leo said. "But to a Nazi, these symbolised the breakdown in traditional art forms and everything that was wrong with 20th century society, not to mention the fact that the artist was Jewish. I'm a little surprised, and very relieved, that they weren't simply burned, along with so many others."

"Remarkable," Harry intoned. Then he recognised the potential scope of their find. "Say, do you think *all* of these crates are full of confiscated art?"

Emily grinned, despite herself. Usually their level-headed leader, she was now as caught up in the moment as the others. "Dunno," she said. "But, I say we find out!"

CHAPTER TWENTY-THREE

ANTOINE AND MATHILDE Joubert
were astounded and not a little put out to
have their third conversation of the day
with members of the Gorey constabulary. Graham's
polite request for a few moments of their time carried a tone of extra urgency as though he antici-
pated some time-consuming, French bluster that he
wasn't willing to deal with.

"*Mais...*" Mathilde began, "you *still* do not
know what happened?"

Graham remained on his feet whilst the Jouberts sat side by side on the bed. Harding took the
room's desk chair and sat opposite them. "We have
several theories and suspects," Graham told her,
watching the woman closely to judge her reaction,

"but we are not yet—not *quite*—in a position to draw a conclusion or make an arrest." He paused his stretching of the truth rather dramatically, his pacing interrupted. "Or *arrests*."

Antoine did not care for this. "I believe, *Inspecteur*, that we have already told you everything we know."

Graham brought out his notebook. Harding knew this as either the prelude to an incisive question or the precise logging of further details. In this case, it was the former. "Did you genuinely think it wise," Graham asked, "when describing your relationship with the late George Ross, to omit that your family owned a small farm that sat directly adjacent to that of George's parents at the time of their deaths?"

Antoine appeared befuddled for a moment. "Farm?"

Harding chipped in with the name of the village.

"Well, yes," Antoine said, stiffly, "but we didn't see how that was important."

Graham blinked at him. "Really, sir? You didn't?"

Antoine was defensive now. Resolutely superior, he was not someone used to being interrogated or accused of errors. "What does this have to do with George's death?" he asked.

"Yes," Mathilde agreed. "What? We can own a farm anywhere."

The notebook flipped closed. "It's not important that you owned a farm, *Madame* Joubert. What *does* interest me is that you were a few hundred yards away when George's parents died. And you omitted to say so."

Mathilde gave a curious tutting sound. "Very unfortunate," she said sadly.

"A terrible accident," Antoine agreed.

Graham turned to Harding who recognised it was her moment. "Would you describe the events of that day to us, please?" she asked.

There was another Gallic shrug, this time from Mathilde. Graham found them intensely irritating. *What do those gestures mean? There's a hearty dose of "sod you" in each one.*

"It's so long ago," Mathilde complained.

"And yet," Harding said, doing her best to ask just what her boss might in this situation, "it must have been one of the most difficult and harrowing afternoons of your life. You comforted a young boy and his sister who had just discovered their parent's bodies following their sudden and violent deaths."

"Terrible," Antoine said.

"The children had all been out playing. George came screaming to our farmhouse," Mathilde reported. "He was covered in blood. It was *'orrible.*" There was a long pause, and Mathilde only continued when she noticed Harding waiting for her to do so. "He was so young, so frightened. His sister was still with the parents, in shock.

Graham recalled that the two youngsters had been thirteen and eleven. A truly appalling experience for anyone, but doubly so for children so young.

"We went to the farmhouse and... Well, there was nothing anyone could do. The shotgun was lying on the floor next to the father. As though he had dropped it after firing for the last time."

"And what did you do?"

Antoine took over. "We had to keep the kids occupied and away from their farm. They took a bath at our place and we called the police. I mean, it was obvious what had happened."

"You are not, unless I am quite wrong, a forensic examiner," Graham heard himself say. "Nor are you a medical professional. How can you possibly have adjudicated so finally in so complex a matter?" he demanded.

Affronted, Antoine stood. "I am also not an *idiot,* sir. The man shot his wife and then himself. A child could have known that." With that, Antoine sat once more. "The police came to the same conclusion."

"That's not how I understand it as told to me by one of the investigating officers."

"What?" Mathilde rasped.

"The children were told that their parents' deaths had been an accident," Graham continued.

"What would *you* tell two young children?" Antoine protested. "That their father had gone crazy and murdered their mother before shooting himself? What kind of monster would say that? What memories and mental disturbances would that leave them with?" His fists were balled now. "You're not a father, I can tell."

Graham let this go. He knew well that a common trick of those with things to hide was to deliberately anger the investigator and distract him from his purpose. It was an old trick, and Graham wasn't going to fall for it. "How do you explain it?" Graham asked. "A happy couple, a loving family. Why would George's father have done something so terrible?"

Mathilde pressed her hands together. "*Monsieur*, we are no strangers to illnesses of the mind, as you know. Our two daughters have their difficulties, and both have expressed a wish, at different times and for different reasons, to end their lives. We know how the mind can be. Life is not easy, sir. The darkest parts of ourselves can't always be explained." Harding was struck by this moment of unexpected eloquence from *Madame* Joubert who, until this point, had remained relatively quiet and stoic.

"*C'est vrai,*" her husband agreed.

Graham found himself at an impasse. He wished to delve more fully into the tragedy at the farmhouse but if he were to press any further, the Jouberts would almost certainly demand that they be provided legal representation, something Graham was keen to avoid. Instead, he tried to buy some time.

"Sir, madam... This investigation is complex and ongoing. Today has been very challenging for us all. We will need to speak with you further so please make arrangements to stay on for at least another day. We'll also be speaking again with Juliette, Eleanor, and as much as is possible, with Marie."

"May we visit her?" Mathilde asked anxiously. "Is she... how do you say... *locked up?*"

Harding fielded this inquiry. "She's not under arrest, but her doctor believes that she needs to be detained for her own safety. She is staying for a few days at a facility on the south coast of the island. You'll be able to visit her there, perhaps tomorrow afternoon?" Harding glanced at Graham, who nodded.

"Very well," Antoine said. "A difficult day, yes. Most difficult."

Graham made a point of shaking both of the Jouberts hands and then ushered Harding out, following her into the hallway and closing the door behind them. He had his finger to his lips and walked with her down to the inn's lobby where they spoke quietly by one of the enormous potted ferns with which Mrs. Taylor had chosen to decorate the place.

"Well?" he asked as if Harding might have gleaned all of the answers by herself.

"It smells," she replied. "I don't believe the murder-suicide story for a second. I think Mathilde and Antoine know more about the deaths of George's parents than they're letting on."

"An astute observation, Sergeant Harding. So, we organise a wiretap and see if they call a lawyer, or anyone back in France, and incriminate themselves, right?"

Harding stared at him. "Huh?"

"Just kidding, Sergeant. Come on, we've got police work to do."

CHAPTER TWENTY-FOUR

THE ART DISCOVERIES, shocking and amazing by turns, had completely re-energised Leo, who gestured expansively with his good arm and gave them all a thorough description of each piece of art. Only two were entirely unknown to him, with neither the painting itself nor the artistic style clueing him in. It was remarkable, Marina thought to herself, that a man with a badly broken arm could even form a coherent sentence, or stand up straight, but there he was.

"We have to assume," he said, "that whole bodies of work were simply destroyed without having been catalogued." He added grimly, "Entire legacies lost."

"But so much has been saved," Harry remarked,

picking up an unframed piece which he'd removed from its crate. "What's this, for example?"

Leo recognised it at once. "That," he announced gleefully, "is the portrait of *Madame* Margareta Knelling."

There was silence. "Who?" Harry and Emily said together.

"She was the wife of some industrialist or other. You wouldn't know her except that her portrait was painted by George DuMarais, one of the most talented Belgian artists when it comes to representations of the human form."

"Kind of a shame, then," Emily said, "that Mrs. Knelling looks like an alien." The portrait was hardly a kind treatment of what was an old and frail subject.

Leo explained that DuMarais was known for hugely exaggerating the features of his sitters, almost in the manner of a caricature artist. "He took what she brought with her—wrinkles, dryness, extreme age, that haughty air she has—and made them the features of the painting."

"Maybe Mrs. Knelling hated the thing," Harry suggested, "and just gave it to the Nazis."

"Doubt it," Leo replied. "It was worth a fortune even then. Now it'd be worth perhaps six or seven million dollars at auction. Can I have some water? I'm unbearably thirsty."

"You need to take it easy," Emily advised him. "You've had a serious injury. I'd hate to think you'd make it worse and end up being unable to play for even longer."

"Yeah, yeah," Leo told her. "But this is a once-in-a-lifetime opportunity."

"These paintings will all see the light of day now," Emily replied. "We've achieved something remarkable down here."

"Yeah, right," Marina said. She had been quiet as they talked about the paintings. "Great lot of good they'll do us if we're crushed to death *down here*."

"It's going to be dark outside soon," Harry said. "If they're searching for us, they might call it off."

"Okay, team," Emily said cheerily, clapping her hands. "We're still in a bit of a pickle, and we still need a way out of it. Anyone got any suggestions?"

They'd already thoroughly searched the room and found it entirely without doors or access points to anywhere else. They were sealed in from all angles. Beyond shouting for help, attempting to dig through the rocky mêlée of the entrance tunnel, or simply sitting and waiting to be rescued, they were out of ideas.

The tunnel was a potential disaster zone. Jagged rocks held up the remainder of the structure. One wrong move and the remainder of the tunnel could collapse, trapping them even further. Or worse, killing them all.

"I can't *believe* no one noticed that part of the basement just came crashing down," Marina complained. "I mean, the noise must have been something else." She was becoming increasingly agitated.

"Apparently not," Leo said caustically. "We're either too deep or too far from civilisation."

"And who's fault," Harry asked next, "is *that*?"

Emily quieted him with a gentle hand. "It doesn't matter. We're here, and we're going to deal with reality."

"Yeah, let's do that," Marina snapped. "Let's sit here and think about how *wonderful* it is that we're surrounded by priceless art, buried under a castle with no one even trying to find us."

"Take it easy, sweetie," Emily put an arm around her, but Marina shrugged it off angrily.

"I'll take it *easy*," Marina growled, "when we have a plan for getting out of here. When we have enough water for more than the next hour. When I'm not bloody starving, Leo's arm can be properly seen to, and I feel confident that this whole lot isn't going to fall in on top of us."

"We're going to have to be patient," Harry told her. "It might even be best to go to sleep for a while. You know, save energy and pass the time."

"Sleep?" Marina shrieked. "How can you *pos-*

sibly think about sleep at a time like this?" She paced the chamber like a caged animal. "They don't even *know* we're down here. There's no way for them to get us food or water. We can't call them because there's no bloody signal. And all you can do is talk about ancient paintings nobody's cared about for donkey's years."

Leo spoke to her softly. "All true. And yelling about it won't change things."

"But we don't have a plan! We're just sitting here waiting for someone to rescue us! Waiting and waiting... We need to *do* something!" Marina protested.

"Why don't you try and get some rest, eh?" Emily tried again. This time she succeeded in wrapping a soothing arm around Marina's trembling shoulders. "Deep breaths, girlfriend. We'll be fine. You'll see." Then she said to the others, "I'm with Harry. Let's all see if we can get some sleep."

In the dark and quiet, it remained only to find a comfortable place. They put together crates, packing material, and sweaters to make rudimentary cots. Within moments, half of the quartet was sound asleep, snoring loudly, whilst the other half wondered whether they'd ever see daylight again.

CHAPTER TWENTY-FIVE

I T WAS WELL into the evening before Graham had a moment to consider just how odd it was that his interviews were taking place just yards from his *own* room. Mrs. Taylor had made sure to give him one of her larger, more recently renovated suites. It had a terrific view of the bay and the English Channel beyond. Now, he noted, it was directly above the room the door of which he was now knocking on for the second time that day. "Let's hope it's a more productive meeting than our last visit," he whispered to Harding as they heard footsteps approach.

Juliette looked much more awake. Her hair was brushed and she had opened the windows. The room still smelled awful, but the blue fog of cigarette smoke had cleared. Graham wondered just how long it would be before Mrs. Taylor made the entire hotel a non-smoking one.

"Again?" was the first thing Juliette said.

"I'm afraid so," Graham answered. "May we come in?" *That Gallic shrug again.* He took a deep breath and pulled up the same chair as before. Harding, following behind, found the room's third seat, and they began.

"I'm starting to think," Graham told Juliette, relieved that the woman looked at her pack of cigarettes on the window sill but did not reach for them, "that to understand what happened to George last night and this morning, I will also have to get to the bottom of events at the farm back in France all those years ago."

"You mean, the accident with his parents?" she asked. Juliette was considerably brighter than before.

"It's becoming obvious that your two families are interconnected in some rather *special* ways," Graham said delicately.

"You think it strange?" Juliette said, glancing at the cigarettes but again failing to take one. "That a man would marry a woman, divorce her, and then marry her sister?"

Graham glanced at Harding. Their new rule was that, upon receiving such a signal, Harding was to ask the next question. It meant a much-expanded role for the sergeant, and she was keen to make the most of the opportunity. "We're not here to judge anyone's marital choices," Harding said. "No laws were broken. But some serious questions remain concerning the death of George's parents."

Now Juliette reached for the smokes. *Bugger.* She lit one quickly with a well-practiced and fluid gesture and then emitted a thin plume of smoke as though she were a leaky industrial pipe. "He killed his wife," she said with a distinct lack of compassion. "Then killed himself. *Non?*"

"Maybe," Graham said.

"Everyone knows this!" Juliette complained. "They were unhappy, or in debt, or had some kind of problem in their relationship. The two children found them dead, and we helped them through it."

Harding decided to go for it. "What kind of relationship did you have with young George? He'd just lost his parents. How did you guide him through such a difficult time? You couldn't have been much older than him." Three years, Harding judged, no more than that.

Another blue-grey billow of smoke filled the room. "It is," Juliette announced solemnly, "a *man's* world." She let this cryptic aphorism hang in the air with the smell of burning tobacco. "Men run *everything*. Look at my father, and then at my mother.

Who runs our family?" Neither police officer spoke. There was the sense that something meaningful was on its way, and Graham didn't want to stem this new flow of information, however characteristically cynical it might be.

"My mother, oh, she might seem strong, but it is all an act," Juliette continued. "She is a little mouse, and my father is a strong, majestic lion. They had nothing in the beginning. He worked and she cleaned. Eventually, it happened for them, but it took *so* long. You think," she asked, "that I wanted to be like her? That I would spend thirty years waiting for my husband to make some *money*, to achieve something, to support me and his children?"

Harding spotted the magic word. "You mean to say... you had an eye on George's inheritance? Even at that age?"

Graham glared at her, worried that she'd spoken out of turn and risked alienating someone who, though stubborn and decidedly odd around the edges, was well-placed to be extremely helpful.

But Harding continued. "His family owned land and property in England and France. They were successful. Everything the parents had would have gone to George and his sister."

Graham was stunned. He'd caught Harding's drift. *You've got*, he thought through a haze of confusion, *to be kidding me.* "He was a boy... Barely a teenager. And he'd just lost his parents most tragically," he said.

"But you saw an opportunity," Harding added. She directed her statement to Juliette. It was a summary of the diabolical machinations of which she seemed more than capable.

"It was a way out," Juliette confessed. "He was good-looking, a nice boy. I would have to wait for a few years but not too many. I was patient. We were friends already. It was just a matter of choosing the right moment to become *more* than friends."

Detective Inspector David Graham had dealt with drug dealers, domestic abusers, tax fraudsters, and crooked businessmen, but Juliette's strategy was breathtaking for its brazen, heedless, obsessive focus on her own well-being at the expense of another. George and his feelings existed solely to be manipulated for Juliette's benefit.

Graham and Harding exchanged another glance. "That's quite..." Harding began but stopped.

"Calculating," Graham contributed. The descriptor seemed too weak to adequately express the extent of Juliette's narcissism.

"Yes," Harding said. "Exactly. Calculating. But you left him. What happened to your master plan? Surely you would have waited until he popped his clogs, or... He had them popped for him." Harding eyed the other woman carefully, assessing.

"I *mis*calculated," Juliette glared at them. "George did not have ready cash, and he wasn't ambitious. He refused to sell his properties. He said they were investments and had sentimental value." Disdain dripped off of her.

"Does your daughter stand to gain from her father's death?"

Juliette's expression brightened fleetingly but quickly settled back into a mask of disinterest. "I don't know. Maybe."

They were all quiet for a moment, deep in thought.

"So do you know what happened to him?" Juliette said, interrupting the silence and stubbing out her cigarette. "Because if you don't, then you're only *playing* at being police," she said testily. "Just *pretending*."

In a sudden surge of anger, Graham wondered, just for a quarter of a second whether he could arrest someone simply for smoking during a police interview. He was *dying* to put a set of handcuffs on this snide, horrid woman and drag her down to the station. But he couldn't, and his lack of a response to her pernicious evil gnawed at him.

"Thank you for your time," he said instead. He stood, urging Harding to do the same. In response,

Juliette turned to look out the window. She did not watch them leave.

Once again, Graham escorted Harding quickly down the hallway before either of them said anything that Juliette or other guests might hear. In the lobby, he stopped and paced around briefly gathering his thoughts. Or perhaps letting his temper cool a little.

"What," Harding offered, "a piece of work."

"Grooming a grieving teenager for marriage," Graham summed up. "All so that she could get a piece of his dead parents' estate." He found himself staggered, yet again, by the seemingly diabolical, selfish, greedy behaviour exhibited by members of his own species.

"But she didn't break any laws that I know of," Harding argued. "At least not *English* law."

"It'd be heartening to think," Graham replied, "that somewhere in some old, thick, French statute book there might be a draconian edict that promises lethal punishment for being a complete *she-devil*."

Harding steered her boss into the quietest part of the lobby. "Don't let her get under your skin, sir."

"I don't know, Sergeant," Graham breathed. "These cases... with families hating each other, conspiring against one another... They get to me. I'm sorry," he said genuinely.

"Want to take a walk?"

Graham was about to agree, certain that the evening sea air would do him some good, especially after the pollution of Juliette's room, but a pair of figures caught his eye. They were moving rapidly through the lobby. *Scuttling* through it, in fact. Their obvious desire for stealth was obvious to Graham, whose radar for such behaviour was unerring.

"*Monsieur* and *Madame* Joubert," Graham said loudly as if announcing their arrival to the whole hotel, rather than their hurried, furtive departure. "What a surprise. I imagine you're heading out for dinner in Gorey?"

The two stopped in their tracks but did not turn to face Graham. At the reception desk, Mrs. Taylor materialised and stared at the retreating couple and then at DI Graham. Her expression plainly communicated the message: *please don't make a scene.*

"But, in fact, it seems not," the DI said, answering his own question with unconcealed relish. "It seems as though you're leaving Jersey." Neither of the Jouberts had let go of the suitcases they were pulling behind them. "And doing so against the strict instructions of the Gorey Constabulary," Graham finished.

Mathilde finally turned and glowered at Graham. "And what is the problem? Why can we not come and go as we please? We are French citizens, under the protection of the European Union..."

"You cannot return to France because," Graham said, in the same annunciatory tone, "you are persons of interest in an investigation into a suspicious death. You are assisting us with our inquiry."

There was complete silence in the lobby. People stopped chatting, early evening drinks were put down with a soft *ping* or a gentle *clunk,* eating was paused mid-chew. "And as such, the only place you are free to return to is your room. Now, please leave your luggage behind and Sergeant Harding and I will accompany you."

Mathilde gave Graham a look that could kill. "Where, exactly?" she asked defiantly. Antoine had kept silent, Harding noticed, deeply ashamed to have been clearly and so publicly caught trying to skip town.

Graham took five paces toward the couple, his gaze fixed on them. "To where this all began. To where," Graham said, his fists balled, "I will find some *answers.*"

CHAPTER TWENTY-SIX

EXACTLY SIXTY-FOUR horizontal yards away from the sleeping musicians, but critically, eighteen yards *above* them, Constable Barnwell was having trouble getting his boss on the phone.

"He's working that mysterious death case, isn't he?" Roach reminded his older colleague. "Which is just a bit more important than this, I reckon. I mean, so far it's just been us two, rummaging around this castle like a pair of twits. Waste of bloody time."

Barnwell got a laugh out of this. "You've changed your tune? What happened to our 'sacred duty to find the missing'? To 'bring home the lost'?"

"I'm tired," Roach confessed, "my feet hurt, and

all I want is a takeout from the Bangkok Palace and a cold pint."

Barnwell did everything but lick his lips. "I'm right there with you. Let's just see what the gaffer says when I ask if we can call off the search for the night." He did not, Roach thought, sound particularly hopeful.

Thirty seconds later, they had their answer.

"No, you bloody well *can't!*" Graham growled down the phone. "You're on a search, and unless they've changed the definition of such things whilst I've been struggling with recalcitrant French witnesses, searches *continue* until they are *resolved.*"

"Right, sir." Barnwell hesitated to end the call.

"Do you need something in writing, Barnwell?" Graham barked. "In triplicate? Witnessed by a Notary Public?"

"No, sir."

"Splendid. Then get back on it and stick to it until you find them."

"Right, sir." There was little else he could say.

"Over and bloody well out," the DI said.

Barnwell slid the phone back into his jacket pocket and then let fly a particularly long, strong stream of invective.

"Wow, Bazza," Roach said, stepping back to admire his colleague's colourful and flamboyant use of language. "I didn't even realise you *knew* that word."

"I know a few more than that," Barnwell warned him. "Okay, no *pad Thai* or cold beer until we've got this wrapped up. And if ever there was an incentive to find four missing prats..."

"Where do we begin?" Roach asked. It was the fourth time they'd been obliged to re-think their search.

Barnwell sighed heavily. "Okay, well first, let's see if that little leprechaun fella is still around and get him to call all the local cafés and bars to see if they are in any of them. It'd be a fine thing if that were the case and we were wandering around here looking for them like a couple of mugs."

"You mean Mr. Jeffries, the events manager?" Roach said. He never tired of giving Barnwell a hard time over his apparent inability to remember names.

"Yeah. Let's get him on the phone. Then we'll sweep the place from top to bottom. Again."

By now, Roach resented this assignment almost as much as Barnwell. The lack of any progress whatsoever had put him in a bleak and uninspired mood. He yearned for the opportunity to do proper police work, the kind of case-cracking, mystery-solving wizardry that Harding was apparently being groomed for. What did *she* have in her locker that *he* lacked? That it was because of her superior ability and greater experience never occurred to him.

They knocked on doors, beginning at the top of the castle where the more expensive guest rooms were located. Most of the guests had left, released from the inquiry into George Ross's mysterious demise, and only a handful of the large, comfortable rooms remained occupied. Nobody had seen a quartet of musicians; even Barnwell's unforgettably vivid characterisation of the beautiful Marina failed to elicit any positive responses. The second floor, almost as empty, was similarly barren territory; the four had simply vanished into the stonework, it seemed.

Jeffries was found, and put to work in his office. He was extremely tired and put out, but hid his exhaustion beneath a thin veneer of cooperation. "I just want to be helpful," he muttered, the dark lines under his eyes testament not only to a stressful day of tragedy and confusion but the taxing task of organising the major wedding which had come immediately before. He called the first place on his list and received a negative response; Roach and Barnwell left him to it and headed into the basement for the fifth time that day.

"Even with the lights on," Barnwell admitted, "this place gives me the creeps."

"Afraid of ghosts, are you?" Roach asked, and then gave an appropriately long and eerie hoot that resounded down the basement passageways.

"Of course not, you idiot," Barnwell replied, with just a tinge of genuine frustration. He didn't enjoy being ribbed by the younger man, especially in these miserable circumstances. Apart from being a less experienced police officer, Roach, an island boy born and bred, could not claim to have lived through anything remotely like the tough and often downright frightening upbringing that Barnwell, a Londoner through and through, had faced. Roach was still a kid, wet behind the ears.

"I know what you mean, though," Roach allowed. "Some seriously grim stuff happened down here. Long-term imprisonment. Torture." They had both read the signage—several times, in fact, during their repeated searches—and were impressed by the depth of the castle's history. They were keenly aware of the stark unpleasantness of life down here for those who'd been unlucky enough to find themselves incarcerated centuries before.

"You've got to be thankful," Barnwell observed, shining his torch into every dark corner, "for advances in the justice system."

"You mean," Roach replied, "that we no longer string people up and burn off their toenails because they won't give us a confession straight away?"

"Yeah, like that. I'm sure it got the job done, mind you."

"Cut down on paperwork, I'd imagine."

Roach headed down a passage, one he knew to be a dead-end, just to make sure, and when he returned to the intersection, he noticed that Barnwell was wiping his mouth with the back of his hand. As they walked together down the next passageway, the older man tried, but largely failed, to stifle a burp.

Roach stopped. Barnwell carried on for three paces, but then stopped too. Neither said anything, but then Roach extended his hand, palm up, his face stern and unyielding.

"What?" Barnwell asked.

"You know bloody well what," Roach told him. "Hand it over."

"It's nothing."

Roach moved toward him and Barnwell backed up a step. "Okay, take it easy," he relented. From his inner jacket pocket, Barnwell produced a small, silver flask. He looked at it for a long moment, almost as if contemplating tipping the contents of the container down his throat rather than surrendering it, but then sheepishly gave the flask to Roach.

"Christ, mate," Roach said.

"I just..." Barnwell began.

But Roach wasn't angry. "You don't..." he began, glancing around rather unnecessarily to ensure they were alone, "You don't have to explain anything to me."

"But I do, mate. It's... you know, this job. I get so bored and down. Like it's all pointless. I don't feel like I'm going anywhere."

Roach gestured to a couple of chairs in a nook near a corner in the passageway. They were placed there for the docents who watched over the castle during tourist season. "You want to sit down for a minute? I need to get off my feet before they begin a rebellion."

The two men sat and Barnwell took a long moment to compose what he planned to say. He was embarrassed; both men knew that Barnwell's drinking had a long history, but that in recent months he'd been doing a lot better.

"I thought with the new boss and what have you," Roach was saying, "that you were feeling, you know, a sense of forward motion and all."

Barnwell shook his head. "It only stayed with me for a few weeks. After that murder at the White House Inn, I thought to myself, 'Good on you, mate, you helped solve a murder.' Felt like a proper cop."

"You *are* a proper cop, mate. You've just lost your way a little."

"No doubt."

"And bloody stupid errands like this," Roach

said, waving a dismissive hand at the great castle which loomed around them, "don't help. Those four are probably in the pub like you said."

Hunched over, Barnwell was silent for a moment. "You know," he began, "I only chose Jersey because I figured nothing would ever happen."

He looked up at Roach who had chosen to stay in Gorey where he had grown up because it was small, the ideal place to show his talents and gain a quick promotion or two. It was also true that to Roach, Jersey was comfortable and familiar, not much of a stretch.

Barnwell shifted in his seat. "And now I'm here, after... hell, is it really *seven* years? Now I'm here, I want to do something *more*."

"Like what?" Roach asked. His shoes were on the floor under his chair and he was massaging his aching soles.

"Become a detective. Spend time with Graham and Tomlinson, examine a few bodies, learn the tricks of the trade. Run an investigation."

"You will, one day," Roach said.

Barnwell shrugged and gave a derisive snort. "You're loopy, you are. The gaffer will have us chasing down bike thieves and the odd tax evader, arresting people for not having the right boating license, or scuffling with their landlord over their annual rent increase. Nothing ever *happens* here," Barnwell complained.

"I beg to differ," Roach said, sliding his shoes back on. "Two mysterious deaths in the last few weeks. Crazy French people and nutty brides. I'd call those *happenings*. Granted it's not exactly *CSI Miami*, and I know we're not at the forefront of this one, but..."

"No, we're in the sodding basement again," Barnwell growled.

Roach stood. "Alright, I'll do you a deal. One more sweep of these haunted passages. We'll report to DI Graham that we've thoroughly searched the place, and are about to become ineffective as law enforcement officers due to a lack of sleep and sustenance. We'll recommend they bring in the big guns."

"Eh?"

"You know, heat-seeking equipment, firefighters, land and sea rescue, if need be. Now that would be a happening."

Rising slowly, Barnwell smiled and gave his friend a nod. "Agreed." He straightened his uniform. "Just one more time."

CHAPTER TWENTY-SEVEN

I N THE DAYLIGHT, the battlements of Gorey castle afforded views of Jersey and the English Channel unachievable from anywhere else. Its position, high atop the only major prominence on this part of the island, was the very definition of "commanding." It would have taken weeks for a major armed force to successfully capture the place. But now, in the dark of a clear night, Graham looked out over the twinkling lights of Gorey and the boats in the harbour and reminded himself that they were not here to take in the sights or indulge in historical musings.

Large, powerful floodlights dotted around the castle added drama as well as illumination to the scene. Graham collected his thoughts as he walked around for several minutes whilst the actors in this particular piece of theatre gathered at the behest of Sergeant Harding.

Rounding them all up and insisting that they accompany her to the crime scene had taken time, presenting yet another point of confusion for Harding on this extraordinary day. There was almost the sense as she shepherded the Jouberts, Juliette, and Eleanor Ross *en masse* up the spiral staircase and through the narrow passageways to the battlements, that they didn't *want* the puzzle of George's death to be solved. Or perhaps one or more of them knew full well there was a murderer among their number and were fighting to keep it a secret.

Whatever the truth was, she knew DI Graham would get to the bottom of it. Or at least she hoped so. This case, only twelve hours old but relentless and intense, was already taking its toll on her and she yearned for the comparatively quiet times they had enjoyed before George Ross's untimely fall.

Graham returned, looking surprisingly energetic as he quickly paced the ancient stonework. "Good evening, everyone, and thank you for coming."

Harding admired his confidence, his way of speaking to a group of people; not superior, or smug, and not like a lecturer or teacher. No, his was the

style of a consummate investigator, someone dedicated to discovering the truth from those who
would prefer that it remain hidden. As she knew
from his performance on the terrace at the White
House Inn six weeks earlier, he was a master of just
this kind of situation. It was thrilling to watch.

The response to Graham's greeting was a col-
lective rendition of that blasted Gallic shrug. "Is
this strictly legal?" Juliette asked.

"We made a request and you kindly obliged,"
Graham told her. "None of you are under arrest."
He couldn't resist adding, "Yet."

Antoine and Mathilde Joubert stood stoically
whilst Juliette leant on one hip insouciantly, her
arms folded around her waist. Eleanor Ross brought
up the rear. She found her way to the front to see
what was going on and peered briefly over the battlements. "Whoa," she moaned nauseously. After a
pause, she crumpled slightly. "Poor George."

"With any luck," Graham told her, "we shan't
be here long. I felt that it would be instructive to
stand at the actual spot from where we believe
George fell and bring together what we know about
his death."

"Know?" Antoine scoffed. "The man *threw*
himself off. That's what we *know*."

Harding fielded this comment, sounding more
like a textbook than she'd have liked but responding

correctly all the same. "We don't have any evidence to support such a theory and therefore can't proceed on that basis." Graham nodded at this neat summation.

"Then where is Marie?" Antoine wanted to know. "If we are required to be here, surely you brought her from the hospital to be with us, also?"

Graham had found it difficult to do so, but the situation demanded exactly that. Marie was as much a suspect as any of them, maybe more so. With a family situation as complex and nebulous as the Jouberts, he needed everyone present, even if that meant requiring the patient and the helpful Dr. Bélanger to accompany her up to the battlements.

"She will be here shortly," Graham replied truthfully. Bélanger had called him moments earlier, assuring him that Marie was, in the doctor's words, "calm enough *at the moment*" to take part in this—hopefully final—stage of the inquiry.

"So what do we do?" Mathilde asked, palms outstretched. "Some kind of stupid pantomime? A re-enactment of something that none of us saw?"

Graham addressed her with a steady gaze. "We establish the facts of the matter," he stated. "Beginning with your locations at the time of the... at the time of George's death," he said, trying to avoid calling it something it might truly not have been.

"I was asleep," Eleanor told him.

"Us, also," the Jouberts added.

"And me," Juliette chimed in. "Too tired and drunk to be anything else."

Harding began taking notes on her tablet, whilst Graham was doing the same, using his traditional notepad and pencil. "And what time did you all leave the wedding?" he asked.

"Midnight," Eleanor said. "There wasn't much happening, and I was tired."

"Eleven or so," Antoine said. "We left together."

Graham turned to Juliette. "What about you, Ms. Paquet?"

Juliette pursed her lips. "I can't say for certain. I had a lot of champagne. I think I danced for a while. Maybe two o'clock?"

Harding made a note, finding at once that this detail triggered a memory. She swished her screen a few times and found the reference in her notes she was looking for. Sam, the castle's night security guard, had told them of a lone, drunken dancer. *Was that only this morning?* It felt like a month had passed, perhaps more. She showed the note to Graham, who nodded.

"So," Graham surmised, "you were perhaps the last to leave."

"I guess so," Juliette said. The others had the distinct impression that she'd been too drunk even to know where she had been, never mind how late it was. "But I was asleep by three or so."

A distant voice echoed from the arch-ceilinged passageways that led to the battlements. "*Mon Dieu*, this is the place where…"

"Marie?" four people said at once.

CHAPTER TWENTY-EIGHT

EMILY AND MARINA sat in the far corner of the strange storage room, leaning against a large crate that remained un-opened. Earlier, most of the quartet had been keen to lever open every container, but Emily had put a stop to their "crowbar rampage," as Harry had styled it. The crate they leant against had been spared the splintering violence of the others.

Emily and Marina had dozed fitfully but were now awake. They had shuffled a few feet away so as not to disturb Harry and Leo who slept more soundly. Soft snoring echoed around the chamber.

"What about some kind of tie-in between the art," Marina was wondering aloud, distracting herself to avoid a repetition of her earlier panicked, hissy fit, "and the string quartets of the time?"

"Hmm?" Emily asked.

"You know, performing quartets by Jewish composers who were forced to flee the Reich. Or maybe stuff by the Second Viennese School." The challenging music of the three greats of serialism—a concept in which all twelve notes of the octave carried equal weight and were freed from the conventions of major and minor keys—wasn't a standard part of the quartet's repertoire, but the idea did catch Emily's attention.

"I like the Berg *Lyric Suite*," she confessed. "Though it's been recorded to death."

"Sure, but never with the benefit," Marina pointed out, "of being associated with a host of recently discovered artwork. Found," she added with a raised finger, "by the quartet themselves."

Emily let her imagination run riot for a moment. "How about a coffee-table book about the art with an accompanying CD of relevant works?"

"I love it," Marina enthused. "We could call it 'Exposure' or something else nice and modern."

"Great," Emily agreed. She shifted a little. The packing material they had assembled was reasonably comfortable, but she was still going numb. "Some wouldn't, but I, for one, kind of like how you're turning this into a commercial opportunity right from the outset. We could use a break."

"Right!" Marina replied brightly. "This could be *huge* for us. And that's before we get into finder's fees and all that."

The thought had occurred to Emily, but she'd put it aside.

"Whatever happens," Emily replied, "it should be equal between the four of us. I mean, Leo was pivotal. He opened that door and later identified the art. I didn't even know who Franz Lipp was, never mind his history and artistic style. But we were the ones who followed Leo in and helped get him over that pile."

"We're also the ones stuck down here wondering if we're ever going to get out alive," Marina grumbled before remembering her earlier resolution. "I can't wait to tell the world about this place. It's going to be... Well, I have no idea what it's going to be like," she added more cheerily.

"Me neither," Emily said. "Like nothing we've ever experienced before."

Marina became thoughtful. Emily guessed she was imagining a bright future where she might not have to scrabble around for gigs and students, imagining instead the luxury of picking and choosing the projects she would get involved in. She was happy to let her have her daydreams and join her in them. The alternative, trapped down in the damp and the dark was certainly not worth thinking about. Then Marina said, "You think one of us should check on Leo?"

Emily shifted again. She was losing the feeling in one foot. "Harry's over there with him. I think he'll be okay." She paused for a moment, "How're you getting along with Harry these days, Marina?" The fling between Harry and Marina had made things difficult for all of them for a while.

"We're fine," Marina replied. "Don't you think so? We're not affecting the group, are we?"

"No, I guess not," Emily murmured. They sat in silence, but something in Emily wouldn't let it go. "But you kind of are, really," she resumed, much more quietly.

"What? How? I don't think so."

"But... it's just that..." Emily began. "You know, I've had... you know..."

"Feelings for him? Harry?"

Emily cringed but accepted the truth. "Yes. For years now. Almost since the beginning."

Marina thought it through. "Please don't tell me that's why you've never married," she replied. "That you were waiting around for him."

Emily blushed deeply in the dark.

"Good God, Emily, if you're in love with Harry, why don't you simply tell him?" Marina said this just a little too loudly. The echo sent her question reverberating around the chamber.

Grimacing and hoping like never before that both Leo and Harry were genuinely asleep, Emily let the echo peter out and then said, much more quietly, "Because I know that it's not me he wants."

Marina sighed. "He and I went down that road. It didn't work out."

"Yes you did, and no, it didn't. But I know that Harry would give anything to be with you. It was just a timing issue."

"Don't be silly."

"It's true! He's..."

"Maybe," came a voice, "Harry might like to decide for himself what he wants."

Oh, hell.

"I'm so sorry, Harry..." Emily started to apologise. "You weren't meant to hear that."

"I heard," he said, struggling up off the ground. He was stood ten feet away, arms folded. "I heard everything, and I want you both to know something."

Neither woman knew what to say. "What?" Marina tried.

"I've been in love with Emily since I was nineteen," Harry admitted for the first time. "That has never changed."

The silence was complete.

"But you know why I've never told you? Why I haven't even asked you out, all these years?"

Stumbling over the words, Emily said, "I don't know, Harry. I had no idea..."

"Because you were already in love," Harry said. "And so completely, so publicly. There was never even hope for me."

She stared at him. "What do you mean? I've never so much as..."

"Schubert," he said, and then ticked the names off his fingers. "And Beethoven, and Mozart, and Haydn. You *idolise* them. There's hardly room in your life for a cat, or your students, let alone a big, bearded cellist like me. I'd have been competing with a room full of dead geniuses."

"But," Emily began and then stopped. There was no way to refute him. She lived and breathed music—especially the classical string quartets—so much so that she thought about little else. It was the sign of a dedicated professional, she would argue. But it was also the sign of an obsessive, a musician so enamoured of her heroes that good romantic prospects and all the rest of her life came and went without her even noticing. Perhaps too, it was a means of distracting herself from what, or who, she wanted but believed she couldn't have.

Emily suddenly seemed fragile, uncertain, and painfully shy. It was not a side of her any of them had seen before. She hesitated, momentarily lost for words. "I didn't know. It's not fair to have kept that from me all this time."

"What would you have done if I hadn't?" Harry asked, still standing, arms folded.

Emily considered this for a brief moment, but it was a decision she'd taken years before. "I'd have said yes, you idiot. I'd have said yes in a heartbeat."

Marina sighed. "Oh, for God's sake."

A weak, but jocular voice came from the other side of the room. "About bloody time," Leo called.

"Enough," Emily chided. Harry was by her side now, an arm around her as they sat together on the pile of old Nazi curtains and sheets.

Marina made herself scarce. "I think I'll open a crate to mark the occasion."

"That's a good idea!" Leo called. "Let me know what you find."

Marina went to him and saw that he was pale but conscious and seemingly in good spirits. "How you doing, champ?"

"Oh, just basking in the reflective, beatific light of someone else's new romance," he said. "I have to say I'm fractionally jealous, but it's been a long time coming."

"Jealous of whom?" Marina asked, wondering if some new admission of long-hidden, secret desire was on the horizon.

"Of anyone who can keep a relationship together," Leo admitted. "I'm bloody hopeless in that department."

"But not bad at all," Marina said, "when it comes to identifying stolen art."

"Sure," he chuckled. "And what a terrific bulwark against loneliness in my old age *that's* going to be."

Marina shone her phone around the room, looking for a suitably large crate to open, but scrupulously ignoring the corner where Harry and Emily were now alone in the dark. *Good luck to them.*

Marina huffed and put the thought aside as she prepared herself. Picking up the crowbar they'd found and weighing it in her hands, she selected her crate, a big one with Nazi text on the side. "Okay," she said to the room. "Cover me. I'm going in."

CHAPTER TWENTY-NINE

THE BEREAVED WIDOW arrived, arm in arm with Dr. Bélanger, but it was hardly a romantic gesture. He had to make sure both that she safely navigated the spiral staircase and that she not bolt.

"This is where... he fell," Marie was saying, over and over. "George..." She had a dreamy, faraway look but was sufficiently engaged, both Bélanger and Graham judged, to become involved in this crucial fact-finding exercise.

"Fell, yes," Antoine said, taking Marie's arm from Bélanger and gesturing toward the edge of the battlements. "Through this gap, perhaps."

Harding stepped across, removed Antoine's arm with a deliberate, firm grip, and gave the grieving

Marie a warm smile. "How are you doing, love?" She and Marie spoke for a few moments whilst Graham took Antoine aside for a stern talking-to.

"It will not help at all," he told him, "to put ideas in Marie's head. I'm interested in the *facts* and *only* the facts."

"She is *my* daughter," Antoine protested. "I may speak with her in any way I please."

"Not when you're all party to what is possibly a murder investigation," Graham hissed. "We should be conducting our interviews at the station, but, if you remember, the last time Marie was there, she became so upset we had to lock her up for her own safety."

He spoke to Marie now, leaving the furious Antoine to stew. "I'd like you to tell us where you were after the wedding dinner was over. Did you go to your bridal suite, here at the castle?" he asked.

Marie thought carefully, tracking the day's events in her mind. "We were married. We had dinner with everyone, and there was dancing." Beyond this, she seemed unable to describe anything. "I... I don't remember what happened next."

"Did you have a lot to drink?" Harding asked. This would, at the very least, offer some explanation for the strange gaps in her recollection of what should have been the most memorable day of her life.

"Not very much," Marie replied. "Two or three glasses, all evening."

"She wasn't drunk," Antoine reported for the record. "I remember her being very clear-headed at the dinner. And she danced beautifully."

"However," came the voice of Dr. Bélanger from the back of the group, "it is possible for alcohol to interact with her medication in ways that might leave her vulnerable to episodes of amnesia, especially under stressful conditions."

It was now Marie's mother's turn to be furious. Mathilde skewered him with a furious stare. "Then *you* should not have prescribed them. Or you should have banned her from drinking."

"No drinking?" Eleanor asked, incredulous. "At a *wedding*?"

This made her Mathilde's next target. "If it was not safe, if it would make her worse even than before, then yes."

Graham quieted her. "That isn't important now. We have a gap in the record that we're trying to fill. There's no indication that George and Marie slept in the bridal suite."

There was no response from anyone to this awkward, if entirely truthful, statement.

"There is a gap of some eight or nine hours between Marie and George leaving the wedding party," Graham continued, "and their next appearance together at the foot of the battlements, just after eight-thirty in the morning. Marie, I ask again," Graham said, facing her, "is there anything you can tell us about those hours?"

Mathilde butted in protectively. "She already told you that she does not remember a thing..."

"I asked your daughter, *Madame* Joubert. Kindly let her speak for herself," Graham spoke sharply.

But his questioning was fruitless. Marie stared blankly at them. "I'm sorry. If I think back, I remember the wedding and the dinner and dancing. Even some of the music. But after that... nothing."

Antoine began to speak in French to his daughter, but Graham stopped him. "English only, please, from everyone."

"Not even..." Antoine translated awkwardly, "the memory of your first night together?"

Marie was shaking her head, staring around as if the battlements themselves might speak up and repair the fissures in her memory. "Nothing. There's just nothing there. I'm sorry. I know that's not helpful. " Marie turned to her mother, "I'm scared, *Maman*. Did I kill George?"

"Shh, shh, *chérie*, it will be alright, keep calm."

To Graham, Marie appeared to have a genuine case of amnesia. It was also true, however, that claiming amnesia was an excellent way to deflect blame, avoid answering difficult questions, and deliberately leave the police with huge holes in their knowledge of events.

Marie's mental condition was either an elaborate plan to deceive or a genuine ailment with a hugely negative impact on her life—and his investigation. For the time being, Graham decided to err on the side of simply believing her, especially having witnessed her all-too-real struggles with her mental state back at the station. But the fact remained, anything could have happened on the ramparts and the intervening hours between the wedding and George's death.

"Okay," he said, taking a step backward, both literally and figuratively. "Let's turn to something else—the history of your two families." Antoine stiffened. "I want to discuss the death of George and Eleanor's parents."

"This again?" Mathilde sighed, but then caught Eleanor's withering expression. "Whatever you want," she conceded with another shrug.

"Take me back to those events," Graham asked them all as Harding swiped to a new page in her notes. "And this time, tell me *everything*.

CHAPTER THIRTY

LEO BUZZED WITH excitement. "So?" he asked for the fourth time. "What have we got?"

"Hang on, Mr. Art Genius, I'm unwrapping the... wrapping," Marina said. The painting was more heavily protected than the others and with softer, more expensive material. "This one has been so carefully crated," she called over. "Perhaps it's the pride of the collection. Ah, I think I've got it." There followed ten seconds of silence which were for Leo an agony far greater than his broken arm.

"Well?" he almost shrieked.

"You need to come over here."

"Really?" he said, beginning to stand.

"Please don't make him," Emily said from the

dark corner she'd been sharing with Harry. "He's not well."

"I'm on my way," Leo said.

"Good. Because... well... you'll see." Marina's voice was tinged with wonder.

Leo held his aching arm to his chest, aided by a makeshift sling Emily had made earlier from her scarf. He tottered over to the crate where Marina was standing in front of her find. "Okay, my little detective, what have you...?" He stopped, stood, stared, and found himself utterly speechless.

The painting was in a large, highly ornate, golden frame. It was of a style entirely different from the modern pieces they'd been uncovering. This was the work of a Renaissance master. Even Marina, no art expert by any means, could see that it was a particularly good one. It depicted a man dressed expensively, clearly a nobleman, but with a certain feminine air. It was as though he had allowed the artist to paint his inner self, not simply the façade he presented to the conservative public.

The subject's hair was luxuriously dark and wavy. His mouth formed a pout. He held his left hand to his heart. There was an undeniable allure that spanned the centuries. Marina thought him very attractive, certainly a seven or an eight; maybe a nine, if he changed his hair or grew some scruff.

She was about to relate this to Leo, but then she

saw his face. He was ashen, as though stricken by some new ailment, and he trembled slightly as she watched him. "Jesus, Leo? Are you okay? Do you need to sit down?"

"Yes," he confessed. "But I'm not going to."

"Huh?"

Emily and Harry came over. "Another weird swirly thing from a guy I've never heard of?" Harry began. "Oh, no... Wait, this is... Well, a lot more conventional."

"That's one way to put it," Emily agreed. "Leo, what have we got?"

His voice was dreamy and uncertain, as though arriving from another room. "I don't believe it."

"It's beautiful," Marina said. "Is it by someone famous, do you think?"

Leo turned to her. "Marina... Harry... Emily," he said, touching each of their arms to ensure he had their full attention. "We're standing in front of a miracle."

"We are?" Harry said, peering more closely at the portrait.

"This is..." Leo could barely say the words. "I believe this to be *Portrait of a Young Man* by the artist known as Rafael."

"Whoa," Marina said, stunned. "You're kidding, right?"

"Jesus, Leo," Emily gasped.

"How can that be? This is a modern collection," Harry added. "This doesn't fit…"

"It doesn't, but it's real, and we've found it," Leo said, holding a trembling hand out toward the painting. "We've found it," he said again.

They watched him commune, transfixed, with Rafael's lost masterpiece for a long moment before Emily broached the inevitable question. "How much do you think it might be worth, Leo?"

Lost in the details of the young man's face, the beautifully decorous accessories of wealth and class, the carefully depicted sable fur, Leo was silent for a moment. But eventually, he spoke. "Well over a hundred million dollars."

Then, with an abrupt folding of his knees and a strange, frightened moan, he collapsed and hit the stone floor with a sickening impact.

CHAPTER THIRTY-ONE

THE TENSION THAT pervaded the battlements could not have been less than that of the castle's hardest-fought siege back in the 13th century. Graham was prowling around the group of five asking increasingly terse questions, relentlessly demanding more detail from each of them. Any pause or error was seized upon.

Harding had never seen him push witnesses like this, but she took it as a sign that he was closing in on his quarry. Or perhaps he was reaching the limits of his patience. She couldn't help but wonder what he might do when that happened.

Graham looked at Eleanor Ross. He was determined to get to the bottom of this case and was willing to assess every angle. "What about you?" he asked. "Were you perhaps awaiting a full share of the inheritance you were earlier forced to split with your brother?"

Aghast, Eleanor stuttered, "You think *I* killed George?"

"You're not entirely without motive," Graham pointed out.

"That's *outrageous*! He was my only surviving family. I would have died for him!"

Graham scribbled continuously in his notebook, but he knew that there was more than an element of theatre in his doing so. Listening acutely, he was absorbing and memorising every word and gesture, adding each detail to what he already knew, analysing and critiquing and formulating his strategy as he went.

The sure-footed mechanisms of his mind, seldom at a loss and frequently surprising even to him, gave him the confidence to be knowingly brusque with these people. If he leant on the right one in just the right way, he suspected, they might simply crack. But Eleanor's reaction was genuine. She would not be the one in handcuffs at the end of the evening.

He had been pressuring them with his interrogations for fifteen minutes now to no avail and he was beginning to doubt his strategy of bringing them together, to this place. He had hoped their proximity and their words would spark a fissure, a split, in their stories or their relationships that would open up the way forward and lead to a breakthrough that would solve the case. So far, it hadn't.

Graham moved onto the scene of the Ross parent's deaths. "So, the shotgun was just lying on the floor by the body of Mr. Ross, the elder," Graham confirmed. "There were no signs of forced entry. And the nearest farm other than yours was well over a mile away. Is that right?"

"*Oui*," Antoine said. Of those gathered, he'd spoken the most so far and had borne the brunt of Graham's questioning.

"Did you check for signs of life?" Graham asked.

Mathilde answered this one, her head shaking. "You must never have seen a shotgun victim, *Monsieur*. There was no chance that either of them were alive."

In fact, Graham had seen more than his share of shotgun victims, but he kept that to himself. "And you're certain," he asked once again, "that this was a murder-suicide?"

"How many times?" Antoine protested. "We've told you what happened. We know what we saw."

"Let me try something else," Graham suggested. "Let's assume it wasn't a murder-suicide. Who might have had motive to murder a relatively wealthy couple?" He looked squarely at Juliette, who said nothing. "Someone who always had one eye on the future. Someone who was determined to move away from her provincial upbringing and see something of the world?"

Juliette spat furiously. "You're disgusting."

"Am I?" Graham asked. "Is it so disgusting to assume that your callous attitude toward human life could extend to murder?"

"I have nothing to say," Juliette told him.

"You cannot think…" Mathilde began, but Graham cut her off.

"*Madame* Joubert, I've known people kill for the most trivial of reasons. Over an old flame or the placement of a garden fence." It was remarkable that the public was so naïve as to assume that murderers belonged in a special, unassailable category of people; that they were born, rather than self-created. He had learnt over the years that *anyone* could be a murderer. And often, they became so for the most slender, even most absurd of reasons.

"So?" Graham said to Juliette. "Why should I rule you out?"

"You are quite insane."

"So no reason, then. Did you ever," Graham asked next, "have cause to disagree or argue with the Ross family, *Monsieur* Joubert?"

Antoine was pinching his nose, exhausted by

the stress of this unbearable day. "They were our friends, our neighbours. We didn't argue."

"In fact," Mathilde added, "we were the same. Politics, religion, you know." She kept her voice mild, almost conversational in her attempt to defuse the rising, crippling tension.

Graham ignored her, pacing rapidly up and down the battlements. "And what about you, Marie?" he said.

"She was good friends with George and Eleanor both," Antoine replied.

"I suggest you let your daughter answer," Graham said. This was just the kind of juncture that was worrying Harding. Would Marie's last, tenuous hold on sanity finally slip under this barrage of questioning? It didn't seem fair to her, but there was no other way.

"We were friends," Marie recalled. "We played a lot together, both at their farm and ours. And along the river and in the fields." She remembered it as a happy time.

Graham stopped. "And did you have the same plan as your older sister, I wonder? A long game, where you inherited the Ross money and land?"

Marie stared at him. "A game?" she said, very confused.

"Juliette already confessed to having planned her union with George from a young age. And not *despite*, but *because of* the death of his parents. Did she concoct this plan with you?"

Marie was trembling now, her head shaking from side to side. "I don't..."

Graham looked at Juliette. "He marries the first sister," he said, playing out his grotesque version of their romantic lives, "and not to worry if things don't work out... we've got a spare!" he announced, still looking at Juliette but pointing at Marie. "All the wealth stays in the family. Very tidy. But there is a problem. You can't wait for him to die of natural causes. So you hatch a plan. Together."

Hands to her mouth, Marie shrieked in mental agony.

"You cannot speak to my patient in this way," Bélanger protested. "She is too ill for this kind of questioning."

"Maybe," Graham said, "but I'm finally getting to the real point of all this. Perhaps what we've got here," he explained to Harding, "is a neat, coordinated, sisterly conspiracy. First one, then the other."

For her part, Sergeant Harding was far from convinced. Not only did she not believe that a pair of human beings could be quite so devious as to plot for nearly twenty years to usurp a family's money, but she thought the two sisters too fragile to murder George in order to seal the deal.

But she also had to acknowledge that there was

some logic to the idea. It explained the twin marriages. It provided motive and the sisters' perceived
mental frailty would help to deflect suspicion.
Could that be it?

Graham pushed forward with a zeal that gave
Harding a flicker of concern. "I suggest that the two
of you conspired to inherit George Ross's estate and
then killed him when you felt you had waited long
enough." He was warming to his theory.

Eleanor breathed heavily in the background
and started to snarl quietly. Marie whimpered. Juliette rolled her eyes. Antoine was boiling red with
unexpressed rage. Janice wondered if this was a
flash of brilliance or a detective so carried away by
his performance that he was in danger of appearing
mad. She was of two minds.

"A conspiracy?" Juliette mocked. "We hardly
even *speak* to each other anymore."

"The perfect cover!" Graham cried. "You two
sisters played a long game, a very long game, almost
admirable in its cunning and tenacity. Why should
I not slap cuffs on both of you and drag you down to
my station, eh? Tell me that!"

Mathilde stepped forward. "Enough! You're
wrong, *Inspecteur*. Absolutely wrong."

Graham backed up and took a long look at her.
"It seems you have something to say, *Madame*
Joubert."

Mathilde shrugged off Antoine's restraining hand on her shoulder. "You will destroy us all unless I tell you."

"Tell me?" Graham prompted.

Mathilde drew herself up straight and stared ahead. "It was an accident, *Inspecteur*. At the farmhouse. It wasn't the older *Monsieur* Ross who fired the gun. It was...," she said, looking at her daughter, "Marie."

CHAPTER THIRTY-TWO

A LL WERE STUNNED into silence except Marie, who was now wailing inconsolably. Graham recovered first. "Pray tell us what happened, *Madame* Joubert?"

Mathilde Joubert leant against a rampart and began to tell her story. "That day, she was over at the Ross's farm and found the gun. She did not know it was loaded. She was just a child, ten years old. She thought it was a game or a toy. *Mon Dieu*, it *was* an accident. "

"Really? But there were two shots. Why, if it was an accident, would she have fired the gun a second time? With one adult already lying dead in front of her?"

"I cannot tell you," Mathilde said. "I do not

know. Perhaps the shock or perhaps her finger slipped."

Juliette moved closer to her father. Eleanor stood stock-still, transfixed.

Harding was speechless but managed to keep writing. Graham rubbed his face for a moment and then said, "And you got creative with the crime scene, making sure it appeared to be a murder-suicide. To protect her?"

Mathilde nodded. "I swore Marie to secrecy. I could see what this would do to her, her life, our family. It was *essentiel* that no one know what happened, and for years, Marie and I kept the secret. Everyone believed that *Monsieur* Ross shot his wife and then killed himself. I thought the... *episode* was behind us."

"But?" Graham asked.

Mathilde took another step away from her husband now, perhaps to disassociate him from the horrors of the past or to ensure he could not move to quiet her. "Marie, my poor girl... Since that terrible day, she has not spoken of it. I think she forgot her memories, blocked them from her mind. To cope, you know," Mathilde looked over at Marie, sadly. "In time, she fell in love with George, after Juliette rejected him." She spat out these last words, casting a vicious glance at her elder daughter. "But she was becoming more and more anxious as the wedding approached."

Marie was on her knees now, with Bélanger's arm around her. The physician was desperate to move her away from this chaos, but he knew that she had to witness its sad conclusion, whatever it might be.

"She began to have nightmares," Mathilde reported. "Very bad. Terrifying."

"And three nights before the wedding, with all the arrangements made and everyone arriving on the island, something happened." Mathilde continued over the sound of Marie sobbing into Bélanger's shoulder. "She was... how do you say... talking in her sleep. About the accident."

Graham put it together. "With George awake beside her."

"Until then George believed, as did everyone, that his father had become depressed and decided to end it all, killing his wife, then himself."

"George woke Marie and asked about what she had been saying, demanding to know if she'd been dreaming or was remembering a long-hidden truth." They all tried to picture such a uniquely horrible moment. "She called me, crying, saying that she thought she was losing her mind. That she'd said something that she could not take back."

Harding imagined George, struggling to deal

with the unbearable knowledge that his bride-to-be had killed both of his parents. "Did you go to their apartment?" she asked.

"I did, and I heard them arguing from outside the door. George was screaming at her... It was very strange of him. But he was so angry, so confused. He kept asking, 'Why didn't you tell me?' I heard Marie explain how it was my idea to cover everything up, to avoid the scandal and punishment."

"And it worked," Harding noted. "Until now."

"*Oui*," Mathilde agreed. "George was a good man. Eventually, he calmed down. They talked and talked. He forgave her. They decided to work together, to trust one another. To go ahead with the wedding. But I worried that, like all men, he was imperfect and fragile. That he might, one day, expose Marie's accident to the police."

"In a way, I felt that they were finished, after her confession. He could destroy her life at any moment. I couldn't let him do that."

"And so, to protect your daughter and yourself," Graham added. "You killed him."

Mathilde sighed sadly. "I had to do it."

"*Maman*?" Marie wailed. "No... don't..."

"*How* could you do it?" Juliette demanded. "How? He was your granddaughter's father!"

"After the wedding, George was overcome. Anxiety, regret, I do not know. He left the wedding and went back to his apartment. Marie followed him. On their wedding night, they did not sleep," she said, calmly. "Marie texted me early in the morning and told me that he was upset. Sometimes forgiving, other times angry. She didn't know what he was going to say next." Marie stared almost blindly at her mother, seeming to have no recollection of this part of the evening.

"They had gone for a walk and were here, arguing," Mathilde continued. "I left our room, Antoine was sleeping, and came to the castle. Oh, I don't know what I thought I would do, but I just had to be here, to make sure Marie was alright, that we would all be alright. I heard him again pleading with her for the full truth, to explain why she killed his parents. Marie just repeated that it was an accident and that the gun went off without her doing anything."

"Except pulling the trigger," Eleanor added, her emotions only barely in check, her fists balled, seemingly ready for violence. "Twice."

"George said something, I didn't hear what and Marie ran off. He was leaning through a gap in the castle wall."

"The crenellations," Graham said.

"*Oui.* He was all alone, his back to me, looking out to sea. I saw my chance. It was so easy. He simply," she turned to look at Graham, "...disappeared."

There was silence for a moment as the stunning revelation sunk in. No one said a word. The only sound was the seagulls circling overhead, their cries providing a seemingly raucous commentary on what they thought of Mathilde's actions.

Suddenly, an angry flurry of arms and a burst of shouting broke the moment. Antoine was blocking a furious nails-first assault on his wife by Eleanor whose forward velocity was threatening to tip Mathilde over the edge of the battlements. Antoine had grabbed her and held her in a bear-hug before forcing her to the ground.

"Sergeant Harding, if you would, please," Graham said.

Harding found her handcuffs and brought them out. Graham nodded to her. "*Madame* Joubert, are you prepared to sign a statement confessing to the murder of George Ross?" he said.

"I am," she said simply and held out her hands even as Juliette tried to stop her, to pull her back away from the officers. "And I am prepared," she announced more loudly so that the whole group could hear, "to be punished for what I have done."

CHAPTER THIRTY-THREE

ROACH AND BARNWELL found themselves, yet again, in the half-completed torture exhibit with the dusty tapestries on the walls. Over the course of the day, Roach had rebuked Barnwell so often for saying, "We've already been in here," that the older constable had stopped repeating the words. On this occasion, however, he couldn't hold himself back.

"The point is," Roach explained patiently, yet again, "the musicians remain unfound, and that means we keep looking *everywhere*."

"Even in dusty rooms marked with 'no entry' signs?" Barnwell shot back.

"Especially there." Roach had checked in with the harassed and exhausted Jeffries whose spate of calls to local hotels, restaurants, and pubs had produced a couple of false alarms, but no string quartet. "I can't help the feeling," Roach shared, "that they're down here somewhere."

There was a tiny movement and Barnwell's eyes were drawn immediately to it. "Hello, what's this?" he said. A slight breeze caused the edge of a tapestry that depicted a battle scene to drift. Barnwell pulled it back, curious. "There's a door here, mate. Still open."

Torches at the ready, the pair eased through the doorframe and illuminated the narrow tunnel beyond. It was filled, from floor to ceiling, with fallen masonry and shattered rock. The two officers looked at each other for a moment.

"You're thinking what I'm thinking, aren't you?" Barnwell said.

Roach gulped as his mind wrestled with this new information. "They're under that lot, aren't they?"

"We'll know soon enough," Barnwell said, taking off his uniform jacket and stepping forward to the edge of the rock pile. He began moving stones to the side with his hands. The pile seemed, at first glance, stable enough to begin the process of moving it and with the musicians perhaps buried underneath, time was of the essence. Or of no import at all.

Roach called Graham but the call went to voicemail. He turned back to help Barnwell lift rocks out of the way, each encouraging the other to move slowly and carefully. Roach was almost sick at the thought of what their efforts might reveal.

"Can anyone hear me?" Barnwell shouted at the pile of rocks. "This is Gorey police. If there's anyone there, make a sound." They both listened for ten seconds, hoping for a plaintive yell from beneath the rubble, but they heard nothing. "We're coming to help you," Barnwell shouted next.

Roach managed to get a call through to the local emergency dispatcher who promptly sent a couple of fire service crews and a medical team. But there was still no reply from DI Graham or Harding. "Honestly, he bothers us all day, and when there's a development..."

"Shut up, Roachie."

The rocks shifted from above and new chunks of debris fell into the gap they had created, missing their feet by inches. "This is bloody dangerous," Roach complained. "We're not trained for this, Bazza. We need to wait for the experts."

"There's no time," Barnwell told him urgently. He tried a new approach, removing rocks from one side of the tunnel and using them to shore up the weakening centre of the pile. "It doesn't look like they're under here. Look, there's a passage on the other side."

Roach reluctantly joined him and they worked together, carefully and steadily. Before long, they had created a slender passageway around much of the rock pile.

"Do you think it will hold?" Roach wondered.

"I don't know, but we don't have time to mess about. Hello!" Barnwell hollered down this new passage. "Gorey police!"

There was a pause, and then they heard it. "Hello! We're here!" It was a woman's voice some way off.

Finally! "Are you alright?" Barnwell yelled.

"Leo needs help," the voice came back. "He's in a bad way. He's breathing again now, but we need to get him out." Her tone was urgent but without panic.

Jesus. "Help is on its way," Barnwell promised. "Hang on. We'll be there as soon as we can."

The two constables stood silently for a moment, then Barnwell started into life. He began the process of levering himself around the jumbled, dusty rockfall and into the chamber beyond.

"What're you doing?" Roach cried out.

"I'm going in," Barnwell replied. "I can't just stand here. They need help."

"But...but...." Roach stuttered, horrified that his

fellow plod was willing to take such a risk and even more horrified that he might be expected to follow.

"You stay here. Tell the emergency crews where we are, okay?"

As he went through the gap in the rocks, Barnwell's shirt instantly changed colour from white to a desert yellow. He coughed and sneezed. There was a grating sound. Dust floated down. Roach jumped back. Barnwell froze.

"Careful, mate. I told you this whole lot could come down." Roach whispered, "Do you want to come back out? You don't have to do this, you know."

Barnwell looked at Roach, sucked in his stomach, and gently eased himself past the pile of rocks and into the chamber beyond.

Once through, he scrabbled over the jumble of rocks to the rudimentary steps the quartet had built and scaled them until he could peer precariously over the ledge and into the next room. He shone his torch around, illuminating the exhausted, dusty trio who were kneeling in the centre of the room, surrounding a figure lying on the floor.

Putting his torch between his teeth, Barnwell, like the others before him, levered his way carefully over the wall into the chamber on the other side.

"Gorey police," he said, very nearly tumbling but finding a handhold on one of the crates beneath. "This *is* quite a find, isn't it?" He jumped down to the floor. "Okay, chaps," he said, quickly dusting himself down. "Everything's going to be alright. How's the lad doing?"

Barnwell bent to give first aid to Leo, strapping his arm more securely and putting him in the recovery position. "Should we make our way out?" Emily asked.

"I wouldn't, love. It isn't safe. Castle's been here for over eight centuries, but it chose today as the day to show its age. Best wait for the fire service to shore up that opening before we make a move. Settle down and tell me what's been going on here. We might be a while."

Outside, Roach continued to try his boss on the radio. After a frustrating five minutes, DI Graham finally picked up. "Sir? We're in the basement of the castle."

"Have you found the musicians?" Graham cut in.

"Yes, sir. They were caught on the other side of a collapsed tunnel. Constable Barnwell is with them now and the emergency services are on their way."

"Good job!" Graham said. "We're all done here."

Harding took the receiver and explained what had happened many feet above the point where Roach was standing. "You've got to hand it to him," she said once the story was told.

"He's done it again," Roach breathed. He pictured the scene. "So he gets everyone together and hits them hard with some ideas, some hits, some misses, carefully getting closer and closer to the target until someone confesses?"

"A sworn and signed statement is being prepared as we speak," Harding assured him. "Are you two okay?"

Roach flicked a glance through the rock opening into the distance where the illumination from Barnwell's torch lit up the tunnel. He grinned. "You know," he said, drawing himself up tall, despite his long, arduous day, "I think we are."

EPILOGUE

MATHILDE JOUBERT WAS summarily arrested and charged by Sergeant Janice Harding for the premeditated murder of George Ross. The case became something of a *cause célèbre*, fascinating audiences on both sides of the English Channel, and giving Jersey and Orgueil Castle in particular, a certain notoriety. At the trial, her defence made much of Mathilde's desire to protect her daughter, who was portrayed as extremely fragile and in need of constant mental health supervision. The jury was not entirely without sympathy but was unanimous in its decision after a ninety-minute discussion. Mathilde Joubert was sentenced to twelve years in prison, a punishment that she received stoically.

Upon release, if thought fit to stand trial, she will be immediately re-arrested and handed over to the French police, who have prepared a case against her for tampering with the Ross family crime scene and lying to investigators.

Antoine Joubert avoided prosecution, persuading the police that he had always believed his wife's explanation regarding the death of the Ross parents and was entirely unaware of her conspiracy to protect Marie. Exhausted and subject to intense media scrutiny, Antoine liquidated his retirement fund and bought a small plot of land on Tahiti where he now lives.

Marie Joubert-Ross was admitted to an institution on the south coast of Jersey known for its compassionate, modern methods of treating mental illness. She made good progress and her conservators are currently negotiating the conditions of her release. The question as to whether Marie's shooting of her husband's parents was accidental or deliberate has not been resolved. Public opinion is divided on the matter. French police are still reviewing the case and have not yet determined whether she will face charges.

. . .

Juliette Paquet was badly shaken by the revelations surrounding her ex-husband's death and has not spoken to her parents since. She returned to her second husband in France, but within weeks, the stress of the case and her husband's concerns that her family was as he later wrote, 'a bunch of nutcases,' brought an end to her second marriage. After brief but extremely bitter divorce proceedings, Juliette decided to make her home in the south of France and now lives in Marseilles. Her daughter went to live with her aunt in England.

Eleanor Ross inherited her brother's estate and adopted George's daughter. After founding a charity that provides support for bereaved children, she met her fiancé, but they have yet to set a wedding date. She is known to favour a very small ceremony close to home.

Emily and Harry married a little over a year after they visited Jersey. Together, they manage the quartet's business operations and have secured several new recording deals and a large number of media appearances, many in connection with the haul of art they discovered at Orgueil Castle. Their recording of the Berg *Lyric Suite* will be released in the spring.

Marina is dating a violinist who plays with the London Symphony Orchestra. She still performs regularly with the Spire Quartet as well as teaching in London. She also accepts speaking engagements about the art discovery on Jersey. She continues to harbour hopes of riches resulting from the find but has sworn never again to open doors marked "No Entry."

Leo is semi-retired from music owing to his injury. He compiled *Dark Art*, a seminal work in which he discusses the Nazi campaign to rid the world of "degenerate art." It also profiles the artists and the stories behind each of the paintings found in the castle. In the book, his contribution to the recovery of the artwork and the group's rescue from the castle basement features prominently. *Dark Art* received international acclaim with the *New York Times* calling it a *"splendid work of scholarship and one of the most important works of history of our time."*

. . .

Stephen Jeffries hasn't taken any wedding bookings for quite some time, but visitors to Orgueil Castle are fascinated by the murder. Alongside nighttime events that focus on the Ross-Joubert case, Jeffries also gives guided tours of the new "Metal on Skin" exhibit, which tells the gruesome story of those who were imprisoned and tortured at the castle. He is applying for other jobs in the events management industry.

What became known as the **"Orgueil Art Haul"** was removed from the castle and conserved throughout the autumn and winter. Many of the paintings were claimed by their rightful owners or sold by the castle to museums. Orgueil was permitted to borrow three of Franz Lipp's landscapes which are displayed in the castle's hallways. The Rafael *Portrait of a Young Man* is currently undergoing evaluation and restoration work before appearing at auction. It is expected to fetch well over $150 million with a large number of potential buyers expressing interest. The precise ownership of the painting is the subject of intense debate. Insurers, owners, and other interested parties are still negotiating the financial aspects of the find, including whether or not the Spire Quartet will receive a finder's fee. Industry insiders have speculated that 5% of the recovered value would be a reasonable figure. If agreed, it would set up all four musicians for life.

Constable Barnwell entered a twelve-step program and now volunteers with the local Scouts. He is studying for the exams required for his promotion to sergeant and has lost over twenty pounds whilst training for a charity walk across Jersey.

Constable Roach met his new girlfriend Lily whilst investigating the case of a stolen lawnmower. He recently scored twice for the Jersey Police in the final of the local five-a-side football championship. He is still awaiting his investigative "big break."

Following the arrest of Mathilde Joubert and the rescue of the musicians, **Detective Inspector David Graham, Sergeant Janice Harding, and Constables Roach and Barnwell** ate a quiet, late dinner at the Bangkok Palace. The following morning, they were all back on duty at Gorey police station. They continue to police the Bailiwick of Jersey with a strong sense of duty, pride, and professionalism.

Thank you for reading *The Case of the Fallen Hero*! I hope you love Inspector Graham and his gang as much as I do. The next book in the Inspector David Graham series continues with a new case that features a missing girl, a broken doll, a scandal some would rather forget. There are painful truths to face. And some people would prefer that their secrets stay buried. Follow the link below to get your copy of *The Case of the Broken Doll* (*Large Print Edition*) from Amazon!

https://www.alisongolden.com/bro ken-doll-paperback-large-print.

To find out about new books, sign up for my newsletter: https://www.alisongolden.com.

If you love the Inspector Graham mysteries, you'll also love the sweet, funny *USA Today* bestselling Reverend Annabelle Dixon series featuring a madcap, lovable lady vicar whose passion for cake is matched only by her desire for justice. Follow the link below to get your copy of 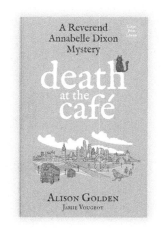 *Death at the Cafe (Large Print Edition)* from Amazon!

https://www.alisongolden.com/ death-at-the-cafe-paperback-large-print

 And don't miss the Roxy Reinhardt mysteries. Will Roxy triumph after her life falls apart? She's sacked from her job, her boyfriend dumps her, she's out of money. So, on a whim, she goes on the trip of a lifetime to New Orleans, There, she gets mixed up in a Mardi Gras murder. *Things were*

going to be fine. They were, weren't they? Follow the link below to get your copy of *Mardi Gras Madness* (*Large Print Edition*) from Amazon!

https://www.alisongolden.com/ mardi-gras-madness-paperback-large- print

If you're looking for something edgy and dangerous, root for Diana Hunter as she seeks justice after a devastating crime destroys her family. Start following her journey in this non-stop series of suspense and action. Follow the link below to get your copy of *Snatched* (*Large Print Edition*) from Amazon!

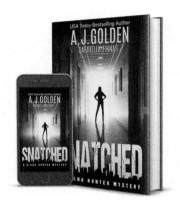

https://www.alisongolden.com/ snatched-paperback-large-print

I hugely appreciate your help in spreading the word about *The Case of the Fallen Hero*, including telling a friend. Reviews help readers find books! Please leave a review on your favourite book site.

Turn the page for an excerpt from the fourth book in the Inspector Graham series, *The Case of the Broken Doll...*

ALISON GOLDEN

Grace Dagnall

USA Today Bestselling Author

LARGE PRINT EDITION

AN INSPECTOR DAVID GRAHAM MYSTERY

The Case of the
Broken
Doll

THE CASE OF THE BROKEN DOLL

CHAPTER ONE

IT WAS A Saturday morning, and it was not starting out well.

Graham awoke feeling groggy, tired, and uncomfortable. In his dream, someone had been knocking repeatedly on the roof of his police car, either demanding help or just trying to annoy him, he couldn't tell which. He remembered trying to open the driver's door, but it was stuck or locked, and so he struggled fruitlessly with it whilst the knocking became louder and *louder*...

"Bloody pipes again," he grumbled, swinging his tired frame out of bed. The White House Inn suffered from an antiquated heating system that struggled to warm the old building, and its pipes knocked and clanged throughout each night. As he started his morning routine, Graham remembered that the same knocking sound had afflicted his dreams for the past few nights, ultimately — in a state that was decidedly unrefreshed. He looked in the mirror, frowning at the dark lines under his eyes. "I look a lot older than thirty-six," he told his reflection. It showed no signs of disagreement.

He showered and shaved as he always did, but he knew that nothing whatsoever would lift his mood until he'd had his morning infusion of high-quality tea. In truth, Graham had never planned to stay at the White House Inn for ten weeks, but the daily pleasure of coming downstairs to the dining room and sitting at his own table by the window with a big pot of Assam or Darjeeling still felt wonderfully indulgent. Every day one of the waiters—Graham knew them all by name now— would bring him a steaming pot of utter perfection, and the day would begin in earnest. His eyes regained a little of their sparkle just thinking about it.

This Saturday morning, it was Polly, a bubbly redhead. "What'll it be, Detective Inspector?" Try as he might, Graham could not persuade the staff to call him simply "Mr. Graham." Even an informal "David" would have been alright, given how long he'd been staying there. But after success with two high-profile murder cases and the recent celebratory article about the Gorey Constabulary in the local paper, his title had become a firm fixture.

"I feel like having something from China today, Polly."

"Isn't that how you feel *every* day?" Polly replied, grinning cheekily and standing patiently with her notepad and pen.

"That," Graham admitted, "is probably a fair comment. Lapsang Souchong, please. And make sure to bring the..."

"Timer. Yes, Detective Inspector." Polly scurried away to place the order and handle Graham's unusual request. There was absolutely no point, Graham insisted, in serving some of the world's best teas if the customer had *no idea* how long the tea had been steeping when it arrived at the table. His solution was to have the waiter start a small digital timer as soon as the boiling water came into contact with the tea leaves. That way, Graham knew when his tea was at its absolute peak. Some would have called him fussy. But on matters of such importance, he knew he was merely being *correct*.

Polly also brought the morning paper. The front page was splashed with reports of the celebrations marking Guy Fawkes Night, the annual commemoration of November 5th, 1605, the day that King James I survived an assassination attempt by a group of English Catholics.

Two evenings earlier, the town had fired off its biggest ever fireworks display. An impressive sum had been collected for local charities, and better yet the district hospital was glad to report only three minor injuries, far fewer than in previous years. Graham made a note to give his team a solid "well done" for their "Safe Fifth" safety campaign. He especially wanted to single out Constable Roach, whose idea it had been.

On the "Announcements" page, there were the usual births, marriages, and deaths—none suspicious—but it was just this relative peace and quiet that was beginning to bother Graham just a little. His first few weeks in Gorey had seen a pair of thoroughly unpleasant murders, requiring the very best from himself and the Gorey Constabulary, but in the last few weeks, their investigative powers had been focused on more routine matters like stolen cars, shoplifters, and the odd break-in. There had been a spectacular case of vandalism at the high school, but even there, little challenge was to be found. The guilty party had obligingly signed his name, for heaven's sake, at the bottom of the colourfully defaced wall.

Revitalised by the tea, Graham set off on the day's errand. He was determined to finish his Christmas shopping well in advance of the annual crush that he had been warned could make Gorey's small shops nearly intolerable. As usual, he assigned a single objective to this outing: a suitable present for his now ex-wife.

"What's she into?" asked the first shop assistant he spoke to. "You know, hobbies? Interests?"

The question stumped Graham. He could hardly confess that he was looking for the kind of gift that might cheer up a woman who had barely smiled in months. "I think she'd enjoy something a little... *different*." When this was no help, he tried, "Perhaps something with some history? With a story behind it?" Graham was met with a blank expression.

The second shop was hardly any better and was even more crowded. "You mean," the female assistant tried, "like something used by a sleb?"

"A what?"

"A sleb. You know, a celebrity, a famous person."

Graham tried again. "Something that is special because of where it has been or what it was used for, as much as for what it *is*."

The assistant frowned. "Nah, I don't think we have anything like that." She bustled off to address a question about Christmas lights, and Graham searched fruitlessly before making his exit.

Further along, Graham came upon an antique shop, and after some thought, he decided to give it a try. "How about this?" the storekeeper asked, presenting him with a highly polished, eighteenth-century pistol. "Belonged to a notorious pirate, that did," he said proudly.

"Anything a little more... *peaceful?*"

In the end, he found what he felt to be the perfect gift. It was a small and beautifully detailed painting of Gorey Harbour, based, Graham was told, on a sketch found in the notebook of a priest who had lived on Jersey some four hundred years before. It showed the castle, splendid and dominating on its hilltop, above a harbour busy with fishing vessels, the old wharf, and a bustling fish market. "Eighty-five pounds," the storekeeper said. "But for a member of our brave police force, let's just call it eighty."

As he was leaving with the painting neatly wrapped in brown paper under his arm, Graham noticed something that he'd overlooked on the way in. In the front corner of the shop's window was a doll dressed in an ornate, eighteenth-century nightgown, with curly blonde hair and blue eyes. Something about it stood out. Perhaps he'd considered one of these dolls for his daughter's birthday one year?

No, that wasn't it. He pondered the doll as he made his way back to the White House Inn, past the three other shops he'd tried. And there in the window of one was a nearly identical doll, dressed the same way, but with black hair in neat braids. It was displayed just as prominently, right by the door.

Moments later, he saw another one. This one seemed older, slightly more worn, and hardly in saleable condition, and yet it stood prominently in the centre of the window. He spotted two more staring out at him before reaching The White House Inn, and as he made his way through the front doors, he saw yet another. On the reception desk sat a pale-skinned, beautifully made doll in a green bonnet.

"Mrs. Taylor?" he asked, his curiosity welling up.

The proprietor looked up from her tablet, which she had been studying with an unusual frown. "Oh, hello Detective Inspector," she said brightly. "Been doing your Christmas shopping?"

"Indeed so, Mrs. Taylor, but I have to ask... These *dolls*," he said. "I'm seeing them everywhere. They must be in half of the shop windows. Am I imagining things?"

She clicked off the tablet and sighed slightly. "No, sir, you are not. But I'm surprised no one's told you about her yet."

"*Her?*"

"Beth Ridley," she said sadly. "Poor thing."

Graham was embarrassed to admit the girl's

name meant nothing to him, but obviously it carried real emotional weight for Mrs. Taylor. "I'm afraid I don't..."

"She disappeared, you see. Ten years ago today. Only fifteen, she was. The brightest, nicest girl you could ever meet. She was well known around Gorey. Everyone loved her. Absolutely tragic."

"What happened to her?" Graham asked.

Mrs. Taylor shook her head. "That's just it. She was walking to school one morning and simply vanished into thin air. No phone call, no sightings, *nothing.*"

"But surely there was a search for her?"

"Oh, goodness me, yes!" Mrs. Taylor replied. "They searched the whole island. All the woods and the beaches. The coastguard patrolled out at sea, looking for her. But all to no avail."

"So what do people think happened to her?"

Mrs. Taylor frowned darkly. "Well, not long after she disappeared, people started talking about her in the past tense, if you know what I mean, Inspector."

He nodded, his lips pursed. "Does her family still live on the island?"

"Oh, yes. Haven't you heard of Mrs. Leach?" The White House Inn's proprietor seemed to have extra time on her hands during this pre-Christmas lull. "The poor woman was beside herself, of course. Her only child, gone. Can you imagine?"

Graham didn't *have* to imagine, but he chose not to share that very private pain. He simply nodded again.

"So, the community rallied around her. Made sure she had everything she needed. Then some people at the Rotary Club, I think, set up a charitable foundation for her. People donated money so that she could keep the search going. She hired private detectives, forensic scientists, even sent experts over to Europe to look for her. None of it came cheap, of course, and I hear the private investigations have tapered off quite a lot lately, but her charity is quite well-known here, and a lot of people give what they can every month."

"Hmm, it's not uncommon for the parents of missing children to carry on the search and at least try to keep hope alive. Even when..."

Mrs. Taylor gave Graham a look that pulled him up short. "Hope springs eternal, Inspector. There are cases, you know, of kiddies going missing and then showing up in some basement years later..."

This, he had to concede. "It's rare, but it happens." But mostly, Graham thought morosely, there was a murderer who had thoroughly disposed of the evidence. Or had got lucky.

There were other possibilities, of course. A child could be spirited away to live elsewhere. Or they might have simply run, never making contact with those they were running away from. All over the country, the filing cabinets of "cold cases," those with no practicable leads, grew in number whilst grieving families were told nothing to ease their pain.

"Poor lamb," Mrs. Taylor said in summary.

"But why *dolls*?" Graham asked.

"Oh, yes, I quite forgot. She collected them, you see. Had quite a number. Her uncle in America sent them to her. She had one in her bag when she disappeared, as I remember. The theory goes," Mrs. Taylor confided, "that the doll was somehow damaged in whatever struggle took place. Nothing but its leg was ever found."

"Its leg?" Graham said, thoughtful. He reached for his notebook but found he'd left it in his room.

She caught him as he turned to go. "Are you going to...? You know... Look into it?"

Graham smiled thinly. "I really can't say, Mrs. Taylor. It's a very old case, and we're short-staffed at the station."

"People hereabouts," she said, leaning in close, "would think the world of you for even trying. Not that they don't already," she added quickly. "But, you know, it would give her family hope."

"I'll see what I can do, Mrs. Taylor. Would you be an angel and keep our conversation to yourself, just for now though, please?" he asked politely.

"Of course, Inspector. You can rely on me."

Graham returned to his room and set up his laptop. Mrs. Taylor had not exaggerated the case's high profile or the extent of public sympathy. There was a Wikipedia page, a dedicated website, and all manner of opportunities to contribute to the Beth Ridley Foundation. Graham began bookmarking sites and taking notes.

As his research deepened, he became engrossed in it, quickly finding himself greatly enlivened on what would otherwise have been just another Saturday afternoon.

To get your copy of *The Case of the Broken Doll* (*Large Print Edition*), visit the URL below:

https://www.alisongolden.com/broken-doll-paperback-large-print

For a limited time, you can get the first books in each of my series - *Chaos in Cambridge, Hunted* (exclusively for subscribers - not available anywhere else), *The Case of the Screaming Beauty, and Mardi Gras Madness* - plus updates about new releases, promotions, and other Insider exclusives, by signing up for my mailing list at:

https://www.alisongolden.com/graham

TAKE MY QUIZ

**What kind of mystery reader are you?
Take my thirty second quiz to find out!**

https://www.alisongolden.com/quiz

BOOKS IN THE INSPECTOR DAVID GRAHAM SERIES

Visit the link below for all my large print editions:

www. alisongolden.com/large-print

LARGE PRINT PAPERBACKS

The Case of the Screaming Beauty

The Case of the Hidden Flame

The Case of the Fallen Hero

The Case of the Broken Doll

The Case of the Missing Letter

The Case of the Pretty Lady

The Case of the Forsaken Child

The Case of Sampson's Leap

The Case of the Uncommon Witness

COLLECTIONS

(*regular print only*)

Books 1-4

The Case of the Screaming Beauty

The Case of the Hidden Flame

The Case of the Fallen Hero

The Case of the Broken Doll

Books 5-7

The Case of the Missing Letter

The Case of the Pretty Lady

The Case of the Forsaken Child

ALSO BY ALISON GOLDEN

Visit the link below for all my large print editions:

www.alisongolden.com/large-print

FEATURING REVEREND ANNABELLE DIXON

Chaos in Cambridge (Prequel)

Death at the Café

Murder at the Mansion

Body in the Woods

Grave in the Garage

Horror in the Highlands

Killer at the Cult

Fireworks in France

Witches at the Wedding

FEATURING ROXY REINHARDT

Mardi Gras Madness

ABOUT THE AUTHOR

Alison Golden is the *USA Today* bestselling author of the Inspector David Graham mysteries, a traditional British detective series, and two cozy mystery series featuring main characters Reverend Annabelle Dixon and Roxy Reinhardt. As A. J. Golden, she writes the Diana Hunter thriller series.

Alison was raised in Bedfordshire, England. Her aim is to write stories that are designed to entertain, amuse, and calm. Her approach is to combine creative ideas with excellent writing and edit, edit, edit. Alison's mission is simple: To write excellent books that have readers clamouring for more.

Alison is based in the San Francisco Bay Area with her husband and twin sons. She splits her time between London and San Francisco.

For up-to-date promotions and release dates of upcoming books, sign up for the latest news here: https://www.alisongolden.com/graham.

For more information:
www.alisongolden.com
alison@alisongolden.com

facebook.com/alisongolden.books

twitter.com/alisonjgolden

instagram.com/alisonjgolden

THANK YOU

Thank you for taking the time to read *The Case of the Fallen Hero*. If you enjoyed it, please consider telling your friends or posting a short review. Word of mouth is an author's best friend and very much appreciated.

Thank you,